All It Takes

A Romancing Manhattan Novel

KRISTEN PROBY

AVON

An Imprint of HarperCollins*Publishers*

ALL IT TAKES. Copyright © 2019 by Kristen Proby. All rights reserved. Printed in the United States of America. No part of this book may be used or reproduced in any manner whatsoever without written permission except in the case of brief quotations embodied in critical articles and reviews. For information, address HarperCollins Publishers, 195 Broadway, New York, NY 10007.

HarperCollins books may be purchased for educational, business, or sales promotional use. For information, please email the Special Markets Department at SPsales@harpercollins.com.

FIRST EDITION

Designed by Diahann Sturge

Library of Congress Cataloging-in-Publication Data has been applied for.

ISBN 978-0-06-289267-6

19 20 21 22 23 LSC 10 9 8 7 6 5 4 3 2 1

For Steve Berry, who is kind of a big deal. Thanks for the balcony plot time. It was an honor.

All It Takes

All It Takes

Prologue

~Quinn~

Five Years Ago . . .

I ease the sexy sports car through the turn, and then hit the gas, smoothly shifting through the gears as the Porsche picks up speed.

It's summer, and late enough in the evening that the sun is casting shadows through the trees as I zoom faster and faster away from the city on a country road.

Away from my family.

Away from death.

I take a deep breath, blow it out, and then shift gears again, my body tense with adrenaline and anger.

Driving fast is the best way to clear my head. Always has been. I prefer it over drinking, drugs, or even fucking a beautiful woman.

This is the only time that I can truly empty my mind and just *live*.

But my sister, Darcy, can't.

And now my father can't.

The pain is swift, leaving me breathless and sweaty, so I speed up further, despite the deep shadows and harsh light from the time of day. I'm racing away to forget, but the fucked-up thing is, I *can't* forget.

Darcy and Dad are both gone, and it's left me with an ache I didn't expect, and a hole that I can't fill.

Even while driving.

Red and blue lights start flashing behind me.

"Fuck," I mutter as I slow the car, then ease it over to the shoulder. I have my license and registration in my hand when the officer approaches my window, his hand resting on his sidearm.

"Good evening," he says.

"Hello."

"I pulled you over because you were driving one hundred ten miles an hour in a fifty-five zone."

I take another deep breath but can't muster up the emotion to give a rat's ass.

"Did you know that you were going that fast?"

"No, sir," I lie.

"Have you been drinking?"

"No, sir." This one isn't a lie.

"I'm going to ask you to step out of the car."

I frown up at him. "I have my license here."

"I see it. Step out of the car, please."

I unfasten my seat belt, then climb out of the car, and stand respectfully, waiting. I know better than to start something with a cop. I don't need to add to my family's stress by getting arrested.

"I'm going to have you walk the line for me, sir."

"Sobriety test?" I feel my eyebrows climb in surprise.

"Yep. You say you haven't been drinking, but at the speed you were going, I can't imagine you driving that way unless you're either under the influence or just plain stupid."

I shrug and immediately walk a straight line, then touch the tip of my nose with my forefingers. I even recite the alphabet backward, only mixing up *n* and *m*.

"Stupid then," the officer says with a half smile and reaches out for my license. "You can get back in your car. I'll be right there."

I sit, trying my best to empty my mind and go numb. I'm anxious to get back on the road, and if that leads to another ticket, well, so be it.

I don't give a fuck.

It's not long before the officer returns and passes me the license along with the slip of paper, giving me instructions on how to pay or show up in court.

"Be careful, Mr. Cavanaugh. I don't know what's eating at you, but I'm not blind. If you do something stupid and kill yourself today, it'll hurt your family."

Bull's-eye.

But I just mumble out a thank-you, then pull away, not speeding like I was, but not turning toward home yet either.

No, I don't want to hurt any of them. That's what this is all about. But I need this, and I have it under control.

I have everything under control.

Chapter One

~Sienna~

Today sucks.

I thought thirty days ago sucked, when we had to bury my grandpa, Louis Walter Hendricks. He and I were close. We did lunch once a week, at the same table at the same diner, where he wanted to hear all about my most current cases. A former attorney himself, he enjoyed the legal banter, and I loved filling him in.

He was wise and funny.

And not a little eccentric.

"Are you nervous?" my older sister, Louise, asks from the passenger side of my Ford Focus. She's twisting her fingers in her lap and biting her lip, and her brown eyes are sad when they turn to me.

"No. Why?"

"I hate courtrooms," she mutters with a shudder, and I laugh, merging onto the freeway from the Bronx, where we live and work, toward Manhattan where we're meeting with Grandpa's attorney.

"We won't be in a courtroom," I inform her and reach over to pat her knee. "You've seen too many movies."

"Where are we going then? Grandpa's attorney works in the Bronx."

I shake my head. "I know, but he wanted the will to be read in Central Park. I don't know why."

Lou frowns. "Wait. We're going to *Central Park*?"

"Yep. Didn't you read the letter?"

"No, I knew you'd read it."

She brushes me off, and I can't help but chuckle. Louise and I are exact opposites. She's carefree, impulsive. Sometimes she's careless.

And then there's me, as organized, structured, and *boring* as it gets if Louise were to describe me. But damn it, life works better with lists and rules. Stability.

I play it safe because just the thought of doing anything else makes me break out into hives.

Not only was Louise named for him, but she is more like Grandpa than I am, and that always made me a little jealous because I loved him so damn much. And she did too.

But my relationship with him was different.

"A will reading in Central Park," she says, shaking her head. "Well, that sounds like him. He loved the park."

I nod and search for parking, which isn't easy in Manhattan.

We should have taken the train, but I have to go to work when we're finished here, and this was just easier.

Until the parking.

"There," Lou says, pointing to a spot, and I slip inside it. We step out of the car, and walk inside the park, our heels clicking on the cement.

My shoes are black, and a sensible two inches. Not high enough to kill my feet, but classier than flats.

Lou's wearing mile-high Louboutins that she most likely charged to her Visa.

I don't want to even *think* about the fact that she still owes me five hundred dollars from last month when I helped her with the rent.

It's not that Louise is a train wreck. She has it together for the most part, and she's my dearest friend.

But she's not great when it comes to money. If she has five dollars in her pocket, she'll spend six.

It's just how she is.

I push that from my thoughts and steer Lou to the area of the park where the attorney said we'd meet. It's near the water, with mothers pushing strollers nearby, and businessmen in suits sitting on benches with their lunches.

Summer has just begun, but the heat is hanging heavily around us already, and I'm grateful when I see Grandpa's attorney standing in the shade, along with our parents and a few family friends.

"Hello, darlings," Mom says as she leans in to kiss our

cheeks. Dad does the same, then smiles when he sees his brother, Patrick, arrive and offers him his hand to shake.

"It looks like we're all here," Dad says, but the attorney, Mr. Mills, shakes his head.

"We have one more party joining us." Someone walking behind us catches his eye, and he nods. "Here he is now."

We all turn to find a tall man approaching. He has dark hair, a square jaw, and he's wearing an expensive suit. The kind of suit that screams money and importance.

His eyes are covered by aviators.

"Who is that?" Lou whispers to me, but I just shrug and turn my attention back to Mr. Mills, who has opened a folder and put his glasses on the bridge of his nose.

"This shouldn't take long," he begins. "Mr. Hendricks has left his home, along with its contents, to his sons, Louis and Patrick. He assumed you'd sell and split the profits, but there's no rush on that."

Both Dad and Uncle Patrick nod in understanding.

This isn't a surprise.

"He also left each of his sons $250,000."

Neither my father nor Patrick's expressions change. Again, this isn't a surprise.

"He left a sizable amount of money to his granddaughters, Louise and Sienna, at $250,000. Each. The remainder of his money is to be donated to St. Andrew's Church in the Bronx."

Louise and I exchange a look of shock. We weren't expecting to inherit any money, especially since both of Grandpa's children are still living, and he spoke often about leaving the majority of his estate to the church.

Not that I'll complain.

"And finally, there's the matter of a piece of property in the Bronx, which currently stands as a park for the community, and has for more than seventy years. Mr. Hendricks has bequeathed the property to the city, with the stipulation that it remain a park for the community to enjoy for no less than one hundred years."

"Wow," I whisper, happy and relieved. This park is an important part of our community. Uncle Patrick squirms in his seat.

"I have something to say," the stranger says from behind us, and we all turn in surprise. "I'm Quinn Cavanaugh, and I am the attorney for Big Box, LLC. Louis Hendricks can't will the property in question to the city because he didn't legally own that property."

"What?" I stand and turn to him, my hands planted on my hips. "He most certainly did own that property. It's been in our family for generations."

"I have documentation that proves differently," he says, taking off his glasses. Brown eyes are pinned to mine, and I feel warmth low in my belly.

Which is just ridiculous because this man is calling my grandfather a liar, so I can*not* be attracted to him.

"He never sold that property," my father says.

"No, he didn't," Mr. Cavanaugh agrees. "But his father did, in 1913, to Reginald House."

"Do you have a deed?" I demand. "Have you done a chaining of the title?"

Quinn's lips twitch, and his eyes narrow on me. "I don't have a deed with me."

"Well, we won't continue this conversation until you have those things *with you*." I cross my arms over my chest.

"If there's an attorney you'd like me to contact—"

"That would be me," I interrupt him. "I'm a city attorney, and trust me when I say, this case will be mine. I'll be happy to meet with you right now."

He blinks fast and frowns as he looks down, then back at me. "I know this isn't easy," he says, his voice suddenly soft, putting me immediately on edge. Does he think he can get his way by playing on my grief?

Asshole.

"No, it isn't easy, but it *is* simple. Louis Hendricks owned that property, and I'll be happy to continue this conversation at a later time."

He nods once, then passes me his card. It's on thick stock, the writing in gold, of course.

QUINN A. CAVANAUGH
ATTORNEY AT LAW
CAVANAUGH CAVANAUGH & SHAW
(212) 667-5555

I tuck his fancy card in my purse before passing him one of mine and Quinn nods, pushes his dark glasses back on his nose, and turns to walk away.

"Well, that was unexpected," Mom says. "Could he be telling the truth?"

"No," I reply before anyone else can answer. I look to Mr. Mills for confirmation.

"I hold an original deed to the property that Louis gave me," he says. "The paperwork is ready to be given to the city."

"I'll take it," I say and then hug everyone, reassuring us all. "This is just another big corporation trying to buy the block so they can build on it. Same story different day, but I never expected that they'd try this at the man's freaking will reading."

"I know you'll handle him," Dad says with a wink as we gather our things to leave.

"If you need any help, just give me a call, kitten," Patrick says before placing a kiss on my forehead. Uncle Patrick is also an attorney, and along with Grandpa, one of the reasons I went into law.

"I'll call if I have questions, but I think this should be pretty cut and dried," I reply. "If I need to, can I get into Grandpa's house to go through the files in his attic?"

"Of course," both Dad and Uncle Patrick say in unison.

"I already have a few boxes at my house," Uncle Patrick says. "I started going through some of his paperwork last week. You're welcome to come get it."

"Thank you. I'll keep you all posted."

Lou and I return to my car, and I'm a ball of anger and frustration as we pull away.

"Who the hell does he think he is?" I begin, my rage finally boiling over. "Our grandfather was a lot of things, but a liar and a thief aren't among them."

"He's just a creep," she says. "But a hot creep. Do you know him? He's an attorney."

"No, I don't know him." I scowl at her. "Do you know how many attorneys there are in Manhattan?"

"Hey, it's not my fault that he's good-looking."

"You shouldn't think he's good-looking," I inform her. "He's trying to take the park away. There's nothing good-looking about that."

"He represents a company trying to take the park away," she says, and I silently concede that she has a point. "He's not doing it. He's the messenger. You're not your clients either."

I let out a gusty breath. "It irritates me."

"I get it, but you need to calm down because getting riled up won't fix it."

"I don't think I've ever seen you riled up about anything."

"I practice what I preach," she says with a satisfied smile, her beautiful face lighting up. "And can I just say that I was *not* expecting Grandpa to be so generous? I mean, he always said he'd make sure we were taken care of, but this is a *lot* of money."

And you'll blow it. I wish he'd put it in a trust, but Lou's thirty-five, and an adult.

I'll pay off my student loans, and have plenty left to remodel my house, and even pay down the mortgage.

"I'm going to Paris," she announces, and I cringe.

See? I knew it.

"I know, it's not very responsible of me, but Grandpa would want me to have fun."

"And a roof over your head," I remind her, but she rolls her eyes, and I don't push.

I pull up to her apartment building and she hops out of the car. "Call me later," she says before slamming the door and sauntering up to her place.

I don't waste any time. I drive straight to my office, files in hand, and begin to research. I can't find anything on record that implies that my grandfather was *not* the owner of Hendricks Park.

Quinn Cavanaugh is full of shit.

But just as I'm about to write it off to another whack job trying to get his hands on this valuable property, I get an email from Quinn himself.

Ms. Hendricks,

I look forward to meeting with you in regard to the property referenced in Louis Hendricks's will. My client would like to set up a meeting for mediation, and ultimately, settlement.

Does June 20 at 2:00 P.M., in my office, work with your schedule?

Sincerely,
Quinn Cavanaugh

cc letter to follow via mail

I scowl and read the email again. He's not going to back down.

And neither am I.

I check the date and reply with confirmation that I have the meeting in my schedule.

I have four days to prepare.

It's hot outside, and that means it's hot inside because I don't have central air in my house. It was built in the 1920s, and no one had A/C back then.

But I love my old house. I updated the kitchen and bathrooms when I bought it five years ago, and last summer, I gave it a new paint job in all the rooms. It's bright, mostly white with a sunny yellow master bathroom.

It's been two days since the reading of my grandfather's will, and I'm no less upset. The anger has simmered down from a rolling boil to just steaming, but I'm anxious to get this meeting out of the way.

And because I'm anxious, and it's a Saturday, I'm painting.

When I'm mad, I paint with oils.

When I'm excited or happy, I paint in watercolor.

It goes without saying that I'm working with oils today. I started a new piece on a giant canvas because I have a feeling this case is going to take a while, and I'll spend many hours working on this particular project.

"I need more red," I mumble and squeeze paint out of the tube onto my palette, then stand back and stare at the canvas.

I'm painting the park, how it looks in the fall after the leaves have turned. It was my grandpa's favorite time of year, and this whole case is about him.

Quinn Cavanaugh would say that isn't true, that it's about ownership of property, and I would normally agree.

I'm levelheaded Sienna, after all.

But not this time. This time, it's about my grandfather, who was the best man I've ever known, and who I lost five weeks ago. He was funny and smart, and damn it, he was *good*.

I won't let anyone say otherwise, and I won't let Quinn's client take the park away from our community.

Not gonna happen.

So I'll paint, and I'll think, and on Monday, they won't know what hit them.

I'M IN THE ladies' room in Quinn Cavanaugh's office building, and I'd be lying if I said I wasn't intimidated.

The building is chrome and glass, brand-new, and damn expensive.

Which I expected.

But I'm a city attorney with an office full of secondhand furniture in a building that hasn't been remodeled since Kennedy was in office.

As in, president.

"You've got this," I say to my reflection in the mirror. I'm in my best gray suit with a black blouse under the jacket. My gray skirt is fitted and hugs my curves without being slutty, the hem falling just below my knees.

Of course, I'm wearing my sensible black heels, and my red hair is smoothed into its usual French twist at the back of my head, without a hair out of place.

Add my grandmother's pearls, and just a touch of makeup, and my armor is in place. I look professional, polished, and ready to make my case.

I march out of the restroom and to a desk, manned by a pretty woman with a headset, talking on the phone.

"That's right, Mr. Shaw is in a meeting until four, but I'll give him the message as soon as I see him." She smiles at me and holds a finger up, asking me to hang on. "Yes, of course. Of course. Okay, thank you."

She hits a button and sighs, her smile still in place.

"How can I help you?"

"I'm Sienna Hendricks, here to see Mr. Cavanaugh."

She types on her keyboard, and then nods. "Yes, I see an appointment with Quinn and Bruce House."

"That sounds right."

"Have a seat, and I'll let Quinn know you're here."

"No need," a deep voice says from behind me. I startle and turn, and there's Quinn, his lips tipped up in a grin. "Sorry to startle you. We're ready for you."

"All right." I glance back at the kind woman. "Thank you."

She winks. "Good luck."

Quinn gestures for me to walk with him through a tall, thick pair of glass doors.

"The conference rooms are this way," he informs me. "My office is in the opposite direction."

I cock an eyebrow, and he just shrugs a shoulder.

"In case you ever need to find my office."

"I assure you, I won't."

I walk ahead of him into the conference room, my head high, palms sweaty, and heart thumping.

But all they see is the confidence, and that's all I'll let them see today.

"May I call you Sienna?" Quinn asks, and I nod in return. "Sienna, I'd like you to meet Bruce House."

"Hello." I reach out to shake his hand.

"And this is my assistant, Kami. She'll be taking notes, and helping out as needed."

The younger blond woman nods, but she doesn't smile. She looks determined, and I like that.

She's not office candy.

"Okay, let's get down to it," I say as I sit and set my brief-case on the floor next to my seat. "I assume you have a deed to show me?"

Both men frown, and Mr. House shifts in his seat.

"I don't," he says.

"Then why are you wasting my time?"

"I have other documentation and an offer," he replies. He's

balding, and his hands are shaky. He's wearing a brown suit one size too small, and everything about this meeting feels *smarmy.*

I don't like Bruce House.

I look at Quinn and shake my head, but he holds up a hand. "Just hear us out."

"You have exactly three minutes."

Chapter Two

~Quinn~

Let me show you what Bruce has with him," I begin and pass a manila envelope to Sienna, then wait as she opens the folder and begins to read. She looks beautiful, and off-limits, in her proper suit, her hair up, and those horrible shoes.

I suspect she'd look amazing in a paper sack. Her hair is strawberry blond, and her ice-blue eyes are more expressive than she'd be comfortable with.

She's smart, and I'm damn attracted to her.

"This is a promissory note from 1913," she says with a frown. "Between Lawrence Hendricks, my great-grandfather, and Reginald House."

"*My* great-grandfather," Bruce says with a nod. "It says that Reginald gave Lawrence twenty thousand dollars, and in exchange for the money, Lawrence signed the land over to Reginald."

"But it also says here," Sienna replies, "that the land would be deeded back to Lawrence when the money was paid back in full."

Her blue eyes find Bruce's and she raises a brow.

"I have no documentation that it was repaid," Bruce says.

"But you also don't have documentation that it *wasn't*," she argues, and keeps going. "And as a matter of fact, I don't have proof that this isn't a fake. It could have been printed last week, for all I know."

"Both men signed it," I reply and watch as she bites her lower lip and gazes down at the paper again. "It's not a fake."

"I don't know that," she snaps.

"I understand that this is a surprise," Bruce says and adjusts his tie. Bruce isn't a bad guy. I don't believe he's trying to pull one over on Sienna; he thinks he's in the right.

Whether he is or not, I don't know for sure, but it's my job to represent him.

"I also know that this property is worth much more than the twenty thousand dollars that Reginald paid for it, and I'd like to make it right."

Sienna's eyes narrow, but she doesn't say anything as Bruce continues talking.

"I'd like to have Quinn file a formal deed, officially transferring the land into my name, and in exchange, I'll pay you one hundred thousand dollars."

She blinks rapidly and sits back in her seat, closing the folder and pushing it away from her. I know before she says anything at all that the answer is a resounding *hell no.*

"Listen," she says, her voice deceptively calm. Bruce nods, smiling with confidence that he's just talked her into his plan.

He's about to be disappointed.

"Bruce, you don't know me very well. If you think that you can pay me barely six figures for a piece of property that's worth millions, all based on a piece of paper that may or may not be real, you're a complete idiot and your attorney should have given you better advice."

That stings. I didn't know about Bruce's ludicrous offer until about twenty seconds ago.

"I'm going to take this before a judge," I say, waving Bruce off when he wants to speak again. "I'm going to ask him to file the deed."

"Based on what?"

I shake my head. "Based on this letter."

She watches me for a moment, then a slow smile spreads over her pink lips and she stands, gathering her things.

"Looks like I'll see you in court, then. Have a good day."

She walks out, and I can't take my eyes off her ass. I'm not proud of it, and I'd never admit it, but Sienna with her strawberry-blond hair and her quick wit turn me the hell on. I wonder what it would take to mess up her hair and get her out of that sensible suit?

Kami discreetly leaves the room, leaving me alone with my client.

"Now what?" Bruce asks.

"Now we go to court."

"She's not wrong," Bruce says. "I can't prove that this letter is real. I found it three months ago, before her grandfather died."

"Did you approach him about it?"

"I tried to, but he didn't reply to my emails."

"We'll figure it out."

"Well, I hope so because Sienna is also correct about what that land is worth, and I'd like to start building on it."

"Don't touch it until a judge confirms you're the owner," I warn him. "Let me do my job, and then you can put a strip mall there for all I care."

"I won't do anything," he says with a sigh as he stands to gather his things. "How quickly can we see a judge?"

"I'll keep you posted."

He leaves, and I walk down the hall to my office, a headache beginning to set up residence behind my left eye.

The first thing I do is call Mom, just to check in with her.

"Hello, dear," she says.

"Did you go to your doctor appointment?"

"It's good to hear from you too."

I rub my hand down my face. "I just want to make sure you had a ride, since I wasn't able to get away from the office."

"Edna took me," she confirms, referring to her next-door neighbor. "And the doctor says my blood pressure is fine."

"I'm glad to hear that. What are you doing now?"

She sighs heavily. "You hover too much, Quinn. Don't worry about me. Work, find a nice girl to court, go on a vacation."

"I can do all those things and still worry about you, Mama."

She laughs. "You always were an excellent multitasker. I'm feeling fit as a fiddle today, so don't worry about me."

"Okay. I'll see you tonight, then."

"If you insist," she replies.

"You don't want to see me?"

"Quinn, I love you, but I see you *every day*. You're allowed to take a day off."

"I'll see you tonight," I reply before saying good-bye and hanging up. I glance at the time and curse under my breath.

I'm late for my weekly meeting with Finn and Carter, my partners and brothers. Finn started our firm just after Dad died five years ago, and we've been incredibly successful. We've thrown around the idea of bringing on another partner, but the truth is, we trust one another and are comfortable with the way things are now.

No need to fix what isn't broken.

"We were about to come find you," Finn says when I walk into his office. Carter is sitting in his usual chair across from Finn, and I sit next to him.

Carter is technically our brother-in-law. He was married to our sister, Darcy, before she died five years ago.

It's a long story.

"Gabby says hi," he says, grinning at his phone. Gabby is Carter's daughter, and the apple of all our eyes.

"I haven't seen her in a while," I say, rubbing my chin. "I'll take her to the movies soon."

"She'd like that," Carter says and then turns to Finn. "Do you have something to announce?"

"What's going on?" I ask.

"I saw a small blue box on his desk earlier, but he was defensive and put it away."

Finn scowls and then sighs. "I'm going to ask London to marry me."

"Why is this bad?" I ask, confused.

"I've mentioned marriage a few times over the past year," he says, reaching for the box in his drawer. "But every time, she just smiles and says *some day*."

"That's not a good sign," Carter says.

"Or, rather than talk about it, she wants you to *do something* about it," I suggest. "Like, propose."

"Well, I'm going to," he says. "At the opening night of the new show she's backing."

Carter and I look at each other and then back to Finn, both shaking our heads no.

"What?" Finn demands.

"I think we've learned a lot about London over the past year," Carter says, "and she would *not* want the proposal to be centered around her work."

"Agreed," I say, nodding.

"What are you talking about? It'll be romantic. I can get up onstage with her when she's introducing the first show."

"No!" we both exclaim, holding our hands up.

"Remember when you decided to buy a house for her, without her knowing, and she was *so pissed* at you? We told you not to do it, and you didn't listen."

"This is different," Finn says, but stops talking when he sees our faces. "Okay, tell me how to not fuck this up."

"You need to do it privately," I say, thinking it over. "Not in front of a crowd of strangers."

"I agree, her whole job always keeps her in the limelight, especially with how well the movie is doing."

London starred in a musical that continues to sit at the top of the charts. We couldn't be more proud of her.

"You haven't had a chance to go away, just the two of you, in a while," I suggest. "Take her to the house in Martha's Vineyard."

"We haven't been in almost a year," he says, mulling it over. "Things have just been so busy."

"It's where you fell in love," Carter says with a smug smile. "I'll send Gabby with you."

"That might be taking it too far," Finn says with a laugh. "But I like this idea a lot. I'll ask her to make room in her schedule for a couple of nights away."

"Perfect. Now, let us see it."

"It has a bow on it," Finn says with a frown. "I don't want to ruin it."

"It's going to already be open when you give it to her," I remind him. "We need to see it."

"Agreed," Carter says.

Finn mumbles something about us being meddling women, making us both laugh, as he unwraps the box and shows us the pear-shaped diamond on a platinum band.

I whistle. "That's one hell of a rock, brother."

"She's one hell of a woman," he says with a grin. "She'll like it, right?"

"She's going to flip her shit," Carter says. "Hell, *I* might marry you."

"You're not my type," Finn says. "Now that we have that out of the way, how did your meeting go, Q?"

"It's interesting," I reply. "I don't know how she'll prove that the money was either paid back, or that the promissory note isn't valid, but that's not my problem."

"It's not often we get a case this old," Carter adds. "It's fascinating."

"I'm hoping I can get in front of a judge early next week. This shouldn't take up too much of my time."

"That's good because we have some new things to talk about," Finn replies and begins going down his laundry list of topics for this week's meeting.

It's late. My meeting with the guys pushed the rest of my day back by hours, but there was no avoiding it.

I'm driving, rush hour long over, to my mom's place, just to check in with her before I drive back to my apartment in Manhattan.

The lights are on in her house when I pull in. I walk inside and smile when I find her in the living room, munching on popcorn, watching the *Real Housewives of New Jersey*.

"I like this Dolores," she says as I walk in the room and bend over to kiss her cheek. "She has spunk."

"I forgot this was your TV night," I reply and sink down into the couch across from her, lay my head back on the cushion, and drape my arm over my face. This is the first moment of the day that I've had to sit and just *be*.

I'm fucking tired.

It's been a long stretch of work, without a break. I'm talking more than six months, working seven days a week.

Maybe I should take a day off this weekend and let off some steam. Go to the racetrack or to zip line. Climb a mountain.

I would say hook up with a beautiful woman, but the only woman who comes to mind is Sienna Hendricks, and I can guarantee you that she would not welcome my advances.

Which only makes me want her more.

I'm a fucking masochist.

"Quinn?"

"Yeah?" I pull my arm away and look over at Mom.

"Did you fall asleep?"

"No. What did you say?"

"If you're this tired, you should have just gone home. This is too far out of your way."

"Mom, I'm fine. I just didn't hear what you said."

"I asked if you were hungry."

My stomach decides now is the best moment to let out a growl, making us both smile.

"I'll make you something," she says, standing.

"No, you don't have to do that. I can grab something on my way home."

"You come here every day, and you don't need to do that either. I'm fixing my son something to eat."

"Yes, ma'am." I smile and follow her into the kitchen, then sit at the table as she bustles about, fills a pot with water to boil, and assembles the ingredients for a quick spaghetti.

"I don't have any of my marinara left, but I have some that your aunt Kathy canned earlier this summer and brought me."

"That'll be great," I say and watch quietly as she makes my dinner. I'm not what you'd call a mama's boy. I can live my life without needing her input, but I do worry about her. Darcy and Dad died within months of each other, and Mom's health hasn't been stellar over the past couple of years.

I'm terrified of losing her too.

So I insist on doctors' visits, and I do hover. I admit it. But if anything were to happen to her, I wouldn't be able to forgive myself.

Not to mention, I enjoy my evenings here, talking with her. Laughing. It's the only part of my life that relaxes me.

"Your father called," she says, pulling me out of my relaxed thoughts and making me frown.

"What?"

She smiles over at me. "He's just going to be a bit late tonight, so I'll save him some dinner for later."

"Mom, Dad's been gone for five years. He didn't call."

She blinks rapidly, then frowns, her eyes sad, as she remembers. "Oh, that's right."

She's never done something like this before. My God, is she developing dementia? Alzheimer's?

I send a quick text to Finn, and then watch as Mom sets a plate in front of me with a sad smile.

"Do you forget very often?" I ask softly.

"No," she says, shaking her head, but I'm not sure that's true. "Don't worry about me, Finn."

"Quinn," I correct her. "I'm Quinn, Mom."

"Of course."

Chapter Three

~Sienna~

I love court days. The hustle and bustle energizes me, and I've always enjoyed a good argument.

Always.

Just ask Lou.

But today, I'm more than a little nervous. This time is personal, not to mention, Quinn will be sitting across the aisle from me.

No matter how often I tell my libido to shut the hell up, that Quinn is *opposing counsel*, it doesn't seem to pay attention. There's a chemistry there that I haven't felt in a very long time.

Of course it happens now, with him. Because that's just my luck when it comes to men. It's the ones who aren't good for me, or that I can't have, that I'm attracted to.

My man picker is broken.

I can't say that I've been to estate court since law school. It's not my area of expertise, and my boss at the city may not like me taking this case. But I've already decided that if we don't resolve this today, I'll take a leave of absence until the allegations against my grandfather are proven false, and things can go back to normal.

I'm not letting another attorney near this.

The judge walks into the room, and we all stand. She announces the case, then looks over to Quinn.

"Mr. Cavanaugh, it's my understanding that you're asking for a deed to be formally filed in regard to the property in question."

"Yes, Your Honor. I have the promissory note here."

A bailiff takes the paper to Judge Maxton, who slips on her glasses and reads it, then looks over at me.

"Ms. Hendricks, have you read this?"

"I have, Your Honor, but I question its validity. I don't know that it's authentic, and if it is, Mr. Cavanaugh can't prove that the money wasn't paid back."

"Is this true?" Judge Maxton asks Quinn.

"The letter isn't a fake," he says. "It's written by hand, and both parties signed it."

"Has it been authenticated?" Judge Maxton asks.

"No," Quinn replies, a muscle ticcing in his jaw, and I know he's irritated.

"Your Honor," I begin and stand behind my table. "I would like to file a motion for quiet title, given the question of its authenticity."

She looks back and forth to both of us, then down at the letter again.

"I'm not going to rule in your favor right now," she begins, and I feel my heart sink. "However, I am going to give you thirty days from today to research and plead your case."

"Your Honor, I don't think we need thirty days to wrap this up," Quinn says, but Judge Maxton is shaking her brunette head.

"This case is a century old, Mr. Cavanaugh. She's not going to find her evidence in seventy-two hours, you need to have this letter authenticated, and my docket is full for thirty days. If I rule now, you won't like the outcome."

"I would argue that I need *more* than thirty days to prove this is fake," I counter, and Judge Maxton raises an eyebrow.

"Fine," she says with a sigh. "It's unprecedented, but given the age of the case, I'm ordering the two of you to work together to find the evidence you need."

Quinn and I stare at each other in shock, then both sit as we wait for her to look at the calendar.

"We will reconvene at 8:00 A.M. on Tuesday, August sixth. Adjourned."

I stand, reach for my briefcase, and am surprised when I turn and see Uncle Patrick sitting in the courtroom. I walk over to him, as he stands to give me a hug.

"What are you doing here?"

"I wanted to hear what the judge had to say, and it's always a pleasure to watch you in action," he says with a smile. "You did great."

"I bought some time," I agree with a sigh. *And now I'm forced to work with Quinn Cavanaugh.* "Do you want to catch some lunch?"

"I have some things to see to, so I'll have to take a rain check. You did great today. Your grandfather would be proud." He kisses my cheek and walks away, and I sit in the chair for a moment, just to gather myself. It really was probably the best outcome for today. The deed wasn't filed, and I have time to prove that this whole thing is ridiculous.

The fact that it's even in question is what makes me crazy. The money *must* have been paid back, if it was ever lent in the first place.

Which I highly doubt.

Now, I have to decide what my next course of action is. I'll go to my office and talk with my boss, Dave. He's smart, and he's always the best person to brainstorm with.

I walk out of the courtroom and come face-to-face with Quinn in the hallway. His client is just walking away.

"Sienna," he says, calling me over to him. "Can I have a word?"

"Just one, I'm in a hurry," I reply and keep walking, my heels clipping on the hardwood of the old courthouse.

"I'd like to get your thoughts on doing some of the research together," he says. I stop in my tracks and stare up at him as if he just suggested we both get naked right here in the hallway.

"Seriously?"

"Judge Maxton is right, there's a lot to comb through. Unfortunately, nothing was electronic in 1913."

"I'm not opposed to taking your calls and helping, but I'm going to research this alone. I'm going to prove you wrong."

He sighs, that muscle twitching in his jaw, and I start walking again.

"Have a good day, Sienna."

"Good-bye, Quinn," I reply without looking back.

"WHILE THE LETTER is being authenticated, you can be searching through paperwork to see if there is a letter stating that the money was paid back," Dave says two hours later as we both devour pastrami sandwiches in his office. "Did your grandfather keep stuff from that far back?"

"His attic is *full* of papers; I'm sure it goes back that far. He was also an attorney, and never threw anything away."

"And it hasn't been touched yet?"

"No, my uncle Patrick said he did get started with one box, but that I can come pick it up from him. He was just getting a head start on going through things, but he's stopped now that this case is in motion."

"Good," Dave says. "But I have to warn you, Si, you won't have many business hours to dedicate to this. We're just too busy. And this is going to take up a lot of your time. We just don't have the man power to give you."

"I know." I take a drink of my Coke. "Dave, I can take a leave of absence. I know this tickles the line of conflict of interest, and I have to dedicate more time to it than you can give me."

"This is shitty," he says with a sigh, staring at his sandwich. "I don't want to lose you and your work ethic for a whole month."

"I will always have my phone on me if you need me, and if you don't mind, I'd like to pop in and out if I need resources or research. Or if I just need to pick your brain."

His lips quirk up in a smile. "My brain is always here for the picking."

"I was hoping you'd say that." I take another bite of my sandwich, relieved that Dave is being such a good sport about all this. Not all bosses would be. "So, the saga gets better."

"Tell me."

"Judge Maxton ruled that Quinn and I should work together on gathering evidence in the case, since it's so old, and we only have thirty days to prove our cases. After court adjourned, Quinn approached me about working with me, but I turned him down."

"Why?"

"What do you mean?"

"Why did you turn him down? This isn't a murder trial, Sienna. It's a property case that dates back decades. I agree with the judge. You both just want the truth."

"Because it's odd, don't you think, for opposing counsel to work together?"

"I don't know, you're both looking for the same information. It might go quicker if you're doing it together."

"I'm going to work it alone, at least to start. I want to prove him wrong without his help."

I don't want to admit that I don't want to work closely with Quinn because I'm so damn attracted to him, and I'm determined to keep this professional. So I quickly change the subject.

"I guess I have to postpone my vacation."

"Just let me know when you'd like to reschedule. Because, Sienna, you're *taking* a vacation this year."

"I know that too. I promise I'll take it. Maybe I'll go somewhere tropical."

He nods and shoves his empty wrappers in the to-go bag, then tosses it in the garbage. "Keep me posted on what you find. Hopefully you'll find something right away that shuts this down quickly and I'll get you back in the office full-time."

"That would be ideal," I agree with a laugh. "Also, I need to look into who might still be alive and can talk to me about what they know."

"The letter is dated more than a hundred years ago. Surely any adults from that time are long dead."

"Adults, yes, but there might be children, or grandchildren, who might know something."

"That's a long shot. You *are* a grandchild, and you didn't know."

I sink back in my chair and wrinkle my nose. "True. But my great-grandfather had a butler."

"Well, la-de-da."

I stick my tongue out at Dave and keep talking. "And the butler's grandson was *my* grandfather's driver."

"I had no idea you came from so much money."

"They lost a lot of it in the Depression," I reply with a shrug. "But the two families were close, and I wonder if Mr. Steve would know anything."

"Mr. Steve is the driver?"

"Yeah, but he's *old*, Dave. His wife, Miss Liz, is a bit younger than him, though, and might remember stories."

"That's all hearsay, Sienna. It's not proof."

"But if she can give me any information, it might put me in the right direction to find the proof."

"Do you think she'll talk to you?"

"I don't see why not." I smile and reach for my phone. "I'll see if I can go see her on my way home from work tonight."

"Go ahead and leave whenever you want," Dave says with a resigned sigh. "Your head's in this today, as it should be."

"You're the best."

"I'm well aware." He winks and leaves my office, and I immediately call Miss Liz.

"SIENNA, YOU GET more beautiful every day," Miss Liz says as she leads me into her formal living room. She and Mr. Steve live in a beautiful home not far from where I grew up. "Can I get you some tea, dear?"

"No, thank you. I just have a few questions for you, actually."

"So this isn't a social call, then."

I cringe. "I'm sorry, but no." I explain what happened at the reading of the will, in court today, and why I'm here. "So, you see, I'm hopeful that you might have any memories of conversations or stories about this from Mr. Steve."

"I've already had this conversation, Sienna," she says, surprising me. She stands, she's clearly irritated, and I am at a complete loss as to what's happening. "If you'd told me this over the phone, I would have saved us both some time. I don't know anything about it, and neither does my husband."

"Did someone come here to interview you?"

Her brown eyes meet mine now, and they're not happy. "Yes, and he wanted to talk to Steve, and that's not going to happen. It'll just upset him. He's been distraught since your grandfather's death."

"I'm sorry."

"You can see yourself out, Sienna."

Liz marches from the room, and I quickly leave the house, hurrying down to my car.

What in the hell? Did Quinn come here and interrogate them? Did he upset them?

Obviously, the answer to both of those questions is yes.

That doesn't sound like Quinn, but I don't really know him that well. If it is Quinn, how did he find them so quickly? As I drive toward my house, I dial his number.

"This is Cavanaugh."

"This is Sienna," I reply and make a left. "I just left Liz and

Steve's house. Liz wouldn't even talk to me about the case be-cause she said she already spoke to *you* about it, and she's not happy."

"Whoa, who are Liz and Steve?"

I frown as I pull into my driveway, beside Lou's car, and cut the engine. "Steve was my grandfather's driver. His family has worked for mine for over a hundred years. I went to interview his wife, and she said you beat me to it."

"I have no idea what or who you're talking about," he replies, his voice smooth and deep. "I swear to you, I haven't spoken with them. I didn't even know they existed."

"Well, if you didn't talk to them, who did?"

"Good question."

I sigh, rubbing my forehead with my fingertips, and Dave's words repeat in my head.

Maybe it'll go quicker if you're working together.

"Quinn, maybe I was hasty to turn you down today, when you suggested we work together." I swallow hard, the words thick in my mouth.

Eating crow is never delicious or easy.

"Go on."

I tilt my head back and forth, trying to decide if this is what I *really* want. Dave's right, I'm a one-woman army, and Quinn is intelligent.

For reasons I haven't clearly figured out yet, I trust him.

I hope I don't regret that.

"It might be worth it if we work on this together," I continue.

"There is a lot of research to do, and at the end of the day, we both want the same thing: the truth."

"You're right," he says. "But I won't have time unless it's evenings."

"I can work with that. Dave, my boss, is giving me a sabbatical until this is resolved, so I'll be working through the weekends as well as around the clock."

"Hold on." I hear pages flipping. "I can make that work. But just to warn you, I usually put in full days on the weekends as well. So it'll be just evenings for me."

"I'll take it."

"Excellent. We might as well get started tomorrow. You can come to my office at six. I'll have dinner brought in."

"No. Manhattan is too far, not to mention, all the paperwork is here in the Bronx. You can come to my house at six tomorrow. Bring dinner."

"You're a bossy woman, Sienna."

"No, I'm practical."

Always practical. That should be my middle name.

"Text me your address. It'll be closer to six thirty by the time I get over there, but I'll bring dinner. Chinese okay?"

"General Tso's chicken for me, please. See you then." I hang up and stare at my sister's car, wondering if I've just made a mistake. I can do this by myself.

But the help will be a godsend. Not to mention, Quinn's easy on the eyes.

Which might be the biggest reason why this is a mistake. Not that I can't keep my hands to myself, because I certainly can.

And I will.

That decided, I walk into my house and feel my eyebrows climb into my strawberry-blond hairline when I see Lou in my kitchen, cooking up a storm, and an army of shopping bags in my living room.

It's a sea of colorful plastic and brown paper bags, covering every surface. Chanel. Bergdorf Goodman. Louis Vuitton. Saks.

She can't afford this.

"Hi," Lou says with a happy smile. She's uncorking a bottle of red. "I'm so glad you're home. I'm making you dinner, and I want to show off all the beautiful things I found today."

"Louise."

"I know, I should have waited until we could go together, but I just *couldn't*, Si. I was too excited, and I found some seriously amazing things."

"Lou, you can't *afford* these things."

"Of course I can." She frowns. "I just inherited a quarter of a million dollars."

"It sounds like way more money than it is, Louise. It doesn't go far, and Grandpa left it to us to make sure we're taken care of, not so you can go buy out Bloomies."

"I didn't make it to Bloomie's today," she says, but I just stare at her, and she finally sags her shoulders. "You're making it a bigger deal than it is."

"The money hasn't even been paid out to us yet. *And* you'll need to pay taxes on it. You don't get to keep all of it."

"My credit cards got a workout today."

"Your credit cards were already maxed," I remind her. Her cheeks flush with anger.

"I got extensions, Miss Goody Two-Shoes." She slams the bottle of wine on the counter. "Why can't you just be happy for me? Why do you always have to point out that you're the perfect one and I'm the one who always screws up?"

"I'm far from perfect, and you don't *always* screw up, but Lou, you can't manage money. You'll have your inheritance spent before you even get it, and then where will you be? Asking me or Mom and Dad for loans?" I use air quotes when I say *loans*.

"Mom and Dad help me because they want to."

I blow out a breath and sit in a stool at my island. "You're irresponsible, and it's time you grow up, Lou. You're too old to act like this. You're not stupid. I don't understand."

"Retail therapy is a thing."

"So is addiction," I snap. "Grandpa never should have left that money to you. You're going to waste it."

"You know what, Sienna? Fuck you. I'm an adult, and I can spend my money any way I like. It's none of your goddamn business."

"You're right, it's not. Until you call me crying because you can't pay your effing rent and need a handout. Then it's suddenly my business."

"I won't be calling you again. For anything."

She gathers her bags and storms dramatically out of my house, and I'm left with pasta boiling over on my stove and something smoking out of my oven.

Awesome.

Lou was making her famous ravioli, the only thing she *can* make. I turn all the heat off, get the bread out of the oven, and take in the mess I get to clean up.

Which is pretty standard when it comes to Lou. I love her more than I can say. Her heart is never malicious. But the woman couldn't balance a checkbook if someone had a gun to her head.

And honestly, I've enabled that, because the tears get me every damn time.

Maybe if she doesn't get any more handouts, she'll figure her life out for herself.

I take a deep breath, and rather than clean it all up right now, I grab my keys and handbag and drive over to my grandfather's house. I have keys and an open invitation from Dad and Uncle Patrick to come and go as I please during my investigation.

There's no time to start like the present.

Chapter Four

~Sienna~

*I*t's six thirty-five, and I'm *just* running through my front door from the office. I'm late, and I'm *never* late.

But I got caught up in legal journals and research, and I didn't get out of there when I planned to. Which wouldn't normally matter, but Quinn should be here any second, so I won't have time to change out of my suit. That's okay, this is a professional meeting, and the more "professional" armor I have on, the less likely I am to climb Quinn like a tree.

I've just shut the door, run to the restroom to relieve my screaming bladder, and as I walk out of the bathroom, the doorbell rings.

I pull the door open and realize that no amount of armor is going to make me *not* long to climb this man.

Quinn's also in a suit, his dark glasses are perched on his nose, and his hair is in disarray from his fingers.

He might be the sexiest man ever conceived.

"Come in," I say and step back, shutting the door behind him.

"The outside of your house and the inside don't match," he says as he sets the bags of food on my island and slips his glasses off so he can look around my space.

I laugh and pull down two dinner plates.

"I know. Not that the outside is *horrible*, but I remodeled the inside before I moved in."

"I like it," he says, scooping white rice onto his plate. "This white kitchen is beautiful, especially with the exposed brick."

"Cooking is one of my hobbies," I reply before stuffing a chunk of chicken in my mouth. God, I'm starving. I skipped lunch. "So good. Hungry."

"I got here just in the nick of time, before you starved to death," Quinn says with a chuckle and eats his chicken lo mein. "Can I have a tour?"

"Sure, we can eat and tour," I reply with a smile, pick up my plate, and gesture for him to follow me. "So I opened up the wall that separated the kitchen from the living space. The house was built a hundred years ago, and open concept wasn't a thing yet."

"No, it wasn't," he says with a grin. How does anyone have teeth *that* perfect?

"I wanted it to be open, especially because I don't have a ton of square footage. So it looks bigger this way. I have a tiny deck out back with a little patch of grass."

I open the door off the dining room to show him, then lead him down a hallway.

"This was originally a *four*-bedroom house."

"How is that possible?"

"Right? It was way too tight. So, up here, I opened the two small bedrooms into one room. I made it so if someone ever bought the place and wanted to separate them again, it wouldn't be difficult or expensive to do, but I needed the space."

I take a deep breath and open the door, then stand back, shoveling rice in my mouth as Quinn walks into my studio.

He sets his plate on an empty table, shoves his hands in his pockets, and slowly walks along the perimeter of the space, looking at each painting that I have propped against the wall.

"Sienna," he murmurs, stopped before a piece I did of the beach at sunrise. "These are beautiful."

"Thanks." I lean my shoulder against the doorjamb and look around at the paintings, including the one I have set up in the corner with the best light.

The one of the park I started last week.

Quinn steps before it, examines it for a minute, then turns to me.

"That's my current work in progress. It's the park. Seemed appropriate."

He just nods and returns to get his plate. "Show me more."

"Okay. Now we're going downstairs. When I bought the place, it was two more tiny bedrooms and a half bath, with a small living space or den."

I reach the bottom of the stairs and turn on the lights to the hallway.

"I reconfigured it. In here is my master suite."

My bedroom is a good size, big enough for the king-size bed. I lead him into my bathroom with a soaking tub, and then into my big closet.

"Wow," he says. "You did a great job in here."

"I love it," I agree, then turn the lights off as we make our way back upstairs. "Well, now that we're fed and you've seen my home, let's get our investigative hats on."

"I'm ready. Where do we start?"

"We need to go to my uncle's house, get a box of papers from him, and then head over to my grandfather's house. All our family papers, going back generations, are in his attic."

He raises an eyebrow. "How much paperwork are we talking?"

"A lot. If we're lucky, we'll find something quickly."

"And if we're not?"

"It could take all the thirty days we've been given," I admit.

"Let's go then," he says. "I'll drive."

I lock up my house and laugh when I see the Porsche sitting at the curb. It just happens to be my dream car, but I won't tell him that. I'll even do my best to not act like a fool when I sit inside.

I can't guarantee that I won't ask to drive it.

"Did you have an early midlife crisis?" I ask him as he holds the door open for me. He chuckles, shuts my door, and walks around to the driver's side.

"No crisis, I just like to drive fast," he says as he buckles up.

"You're driving the right car then," I reply and run my hand over the leather. It's like butter. "I admit, it's beautiful."

"She's fucking amazing," he says with a smile and pulls away from the curb. I give him directions to Uncle Patrick's house and smile the whole way there.

Yes, he drives too fast, but it's thrilling. I'd never have the guts to do it.

"Here we are," I say when he pulls into the driveway. Before I can suggest that I'll go by myself, he unbuckles his seat belt, jumps out of the car, and opens my door. "This isn't a date."

"So?"

"So you don't need to open doors for me."

"Are you one of those women who's offended when a man opens a door for her?"

"No, of course not. I'm just reminding you that we're not dating."

"Sienna, I'm a gentleman, whether on a date or opening a door for a stranger at the courthouse. It doesn't mean any more than that."

"Well, okay then." I smooth my jacket and walk ahead of him, up the steps to Uncle Patrick's front door. He answers, and smiles at us, surprised to see Quinn.

I make the introductions, and Uncle Patrick passes the box of paperwork to Quinn.

"Here you go. I hope you find what you're looking for."

"Me too," I reply.

"Just call if you need anything."

He shuts the door, not inviting us inside, which seems a little out of character, but I brush it off. Quinn is a stranger, and we have work to do.

Once inside Quinn's sexy car, we don't have far to go to get to my grandfather's house.

"You all live close together," Quinn says when he pulls into the driveway.

"Always have," I agree with a nod. "Our family is superclose. I like living near them, in case they need me."

"I get it," he says as I unlock the front door. He follows me inside and sets the box down as I flip on lights and take a look around. "I'm close to my family as well."

"I came by last night to get the attic cleaned up a bit so we aren't sitting in dirt."

I lead him up the stairs to the second floor, then open a door that leads to another staircase, up to the attic. I turn on the lights and Quinn follows me up the steps.

"I was always so scared to come up here when I was a kid," I admit with a chuckle. "Go ahead and set that down any-where. As you can see, I moved the boxes to the perimeter of the room, so we can sit in the middle and start sifting through them."

"Why did it scare you up here?" he asks and crosses to me, brushing a loose piece of hair off my cheek.

"Spooky attic," I reply with a shrug, my cheek vibrating

from his touch. "Maybe I read too many *Goosebumps* books as a kid."

"I don't think there's anything up here that can hurt you."

"Well, there could be something in these boxes that could do some damage, but there are no ghosts," I reply and reach for a box, then sit on the floor and open the lid. "Although, there's also no air-conditioning up here."

"Take off your jacket," he says as he removes his own, folds it in half, and lays it over an old chair. He loosens his tie, takes that off as well, and unbuttons his shirt, then rolls his sleeves halfway up his forearms. "That's better."

"I'm fine."

I clear my throat and look in the box. It's full of old, musty, yellowed papers.

"So are you and Patrick close?"

"Yeah, always have been," I reply, pulling out receipts from 1952. "Wow, they paid five cents for a loaf of bread. I really need to focus. No reading everything, even though it's so interesting."

"If we get caught up in the price of bread, it'll take us six months to get through this," Quinn agrees. "I'd say we're looking for handwritten notes, since that's how the original was written. And it could be anywhere, but I'll focus on files. If your grandfathers were attorneys, there's a good chance they filed this, especially given the gravity of the matter."

"Good thinking. I'll concentrate on the same, but I will quickly scan each paper to make sure it's not what we need, and not get focused on the contents otherwise." I nod decisively and begin to dig. "So, anyway, Uncle Patrick and I have always been close. He's also an attorney."

Quinn just nods and keeps reading through papers.

"Why?"

His gaze whips up to mine. "Why what?"

"Why do you ask?"

"I was just curious."

He looks down again, and I frown. Rather than question him, I dig back into the box and shift on the floor. I'm hot and uncomfortable, and wishing for cooler clothes.

"Take your jacket off," Quinn repeats, not looking up from the paper he's reading. "You'll feel better."

I sigh, shrug a shoulder, and wrestle my way out of the jacket, then kick my two-inch shoes off for good measure and wiggle my toes.

Okay, he was right. I *do* feel better.

"See?"

"I'll bring a fan tomorrow."

"Is anyone living here?" he asks.

"No."

"Why don't I just carry the boxes downstairs, a few at a time, and we can work at the table where it's cooler and more comfortable."

"They're heavy."

His brown eyes stay on mine, not flinching, and I can't help but laugh.

"Okay, muscleman, if you want to carry the heavy boxes, who am I to stop you? It will be more comfortable, and I'll be closer to the coffeepot and fridge when I'm here all by myself and need fuel."

"You'll be here alone?"

He's scowling.

"Of course. You'll be working during the day on the weekends, and I still have to find my proof. It's no big deal. I've been home alone before. You know, because I'm a grown-up."

He rolls his eyes and closes the lid on his finished box, then moves it to the other side of the room under a paper I taped to the wall that says *FINISHED*.

He pulls his phone out of his pocket. "I need to make a quick call."

"Of course."

I also put the lid on my box, a bit disappointed that I didn't find what I needed right away, and reach for another.

"Hi, Mom. I just wanted to check in. I don't think I'm going to make it over tonight." He pauses, listening, a smile hovering over his lips. "Yes, you're on a Quinn vacation tonight. You're funny. Are you feeling okay? Good. I'll talk to you tomorrow. Good night."

"If you need to go to your mom's, you don't have to stay—"

"I don't," he replies, tucking his phone back in his pocket.

"Are you a mama's boy?" My voice is taunting, playful. Quinn chuckles, shakes his head, and takes my finished box to join his.

"No. I do love my mom, though, and my family would say that I'm overprotective. My sister and dad both died in the same year about five years ago, and ever since then I keep a close eye on Mom."

"I'm sorry," I murmur, watching his jaw tighten as he reaches for another box.

"So I understand being close to your family. I enjoy being around mine."

"Do you live close to them?"

"To Finn, yes. He's my older brother, and he and I both have condos in Manhattan, not far from the office."

Sweat breaks out on my upper lip. Condos in Manhattan are not cheap.

"Mom and Carter live in Queens."

"Who's Carter?"

"He's my brother-in-law. He was married to my sister, and he's the third partner in our firm."

"Any other siblings?" I ask.

"Nope, it's just the three of us. Carter and Darcy have a daughter, Gabby, who's twelve and a handful."

"Twelve is the new twenty-five," I agree with a laugh. "It's great that you work with your brothers."

"We trust one another, and we get along well, so it works for us. Sometimes we get on each other's nerves, but that's family for you."

"Absolutely."

"What about you?"

"I have a sister."

"No, I mean, tell me about why you're a city attorney, and not working with a private firm. You have to know that you could be making much more money."

"I know, but that's not why I do this, you know?"

He just shakes his head, and I shrug a shoulder. "I'm not a martyr. Of course I work for the money. If I didn't need money, I'd retire and go live on a beach somewhere. But I also don't want to be married to the work.

"You admitted to me that you work seven days a week. I don't want that, Quinn. I work Monday through Friday, eight to five. There are a few days here and there that I stay a little late, if I'm preparing for court, but for the most part, it's forty hours a week. I don't have to count billable hours, accounting for every fifteen minutes of my day. I'm on a decent salary. And in exchange, I can have a life. I paint, I cook, I can be with my family. I honestly don't know how or why *you* want to work so hard."

"It's the thrill," he admits. "I fucking love a courtroom. I will always be a litigator because it makes my heart beat."

"Then we're both doing what we want to do," I reply with a smile. "I'm not a workaholic, and I'm okay with that. It doesn't mean that my work ethic isn't stellar. I work my ass off. But I like having a life outside of it. I *need* it."

"I can see that from your artwork. You're incredibly talented."

"Thank you."

"Have you ever sold any?"

"Yes."

This seems to surprise him, and I smile as I put the lid on another box that didn't give me any answers.

"I've even had exhibits in some smaller galleries. I can't keep it all, and my family only has so much wall space."

"Good point," he says, shoving both of our boxes in the finished pile. "I'd like to buy that beach painting, if it's for sale."

"It's not." Actually, that's a lie. It's totally for sale, but I don't feel right about selling it to him. "But I'd like to give it to you."

"I'm happy to pay for it."

"And I'm happy to give it to you," I repeat, standing and brushing my skirt before slipping my feet into my shoes. "And if you don't mind, I think I'm done for the night."

"That's fine with me. I'll take you home."

Quinn takes a half-dozen boxes down to the dining room while I turn off the lights, and he waits as I lock the house up, then we drive toward my house. My phone rings in my lap.

"Ugh, it's Lou." I reject the call and drop my phone in my bag.

"You don't like him?"

"It's a her," I reply with a smile. "Louise is my sister, and I love her, but I'm mad at her right now."

I explain just the surface of our fight, not getting too deep into Louise's financial issues.

"So, you know. Family drama."

"I do know about family drama," he replies with a laugh. "You'll figure it out."

He pulls into my driveway and follows me to the door.

"I'll get the painting for you."

"Sienna, let me pay for it. Really. I don't want it to be a conflict of interest."

I unlock the door, we step inside, and I turn to him. "I saw the way you looked at it. It touched you, and I don't need to know the reasons why. As an artist, seeing that look on someone's face when they look at my work, well, it makes me happy. It'll have a good home, and that's *not* a conflict of interest. It's being a nice human being, giving my art to another human being who appreciates it."

He reaches up and brushes his thumb over my cheek, and I won't even begin to list all the ways I *am* feeling like this is a conflict of interest with the way my libido is in overdrive whenever I'm with him.

"You had some dust here."

"Dusty attic," I whisper, then pull away. "I'll be right back."

I kick my shoes off and march back to my studio and quickly wrap the painting in plastic so it survives the ride home, then return to him.

"Thank you," he says as he takes it from me. "I know just where I'll hang it."

"You're welcome."

He cups my cheek now, and I'm sure he's going to kiss me. This is *not* professional, and I should back away.

But I can't.

And he doesn't kiss me.

At least, not on the lips.

He presses those sexy lips against my forehead, takes a deep breath, and then he's gone and I'm left with raging lust.

Chapter Five

~Quinn~

That was the *best*," Gabby says on Saturday afternoon as we leave the early matinee of the newest Pixar film. I was at the office by six this morning to get some work done before picking my niece up for our date. "It was funny."

"I liked it too," I reply and kiss her dark head.

"We should go out to lunch now," she says with a grin, and I pull her against my side for a hug. "I'm starving."

"You just devoured a large popcorn, had a soda, and ate a box of peanut M&M's by yourself."

"So?" She bats her eyelashes at me, making me laugh.

"As much as I would love to, I can't. I have to go to work. But we can pick up anything you want on our way to your house."

"Okay," she says with a shrug. "I want pastrami."

Our favorite sandwich shop isn't far, and before long we're

loaded down with sandwiches for Gabby and Carter, and more for Sienna and myself.

"Thanks for today, Uncle Quinn," Gabby says as we get out of the car and I walk her to the door, carrying her food.

"Anytime, buttercup," I reply as Carter opens the door. "We brought food."

"Thanks, come on in. Did you have fun, Gabs?"

"Yeah," she says. "But Uncle Quinn can't stay."

Carter's eyes meet mine as I hand him the brown bag full of lunch.

"I have to go to work," I say. "She was great. We had a good time."

"Good. Thanks for taking her."

"It's always my pleasure. I'll see you Monday."

I hurry back to my car, looking forward to seeing Sienna today. I wasn't able to make it over yesterday because work took longer than I anticipated, and I wanted to clear my calendar for this afternoon so I could spend time with Gabby and go help Sienna.

Not to mention, I wanted tomorrow off from the office as well. I need some time at the track, and I'm going to talk Sienna into going with me.

I don't know how, but I'll figure it out.

Traffic isn't too horrible for a Saturday afternoon, and before long I'm in the Bronx, driving toward Louis Hendricks's former home. Sienna's already there.

I pull in behind her silver Ford, lock the car, and ring the doorbell.

Sienna opens the door, and I feel like my tongue is suddenly permanently stuck to the roof of my mouth.

Holy God almighty.

She's not in her suit and sensible heels today.

Not even close.

Her hair, usually back in a sleek French twist, is pulled up in a messy bun with tendrils falling around her face and neck. She's in a black tank top and cutoff shorts.

Her long legs are bare, as are her feet.

But the kicker? There's not a speck of makeup on her and she's wearing black-rimmed glasses, and I'm instantly turned on.

I swallow hard as she backs away from the door, already talking, but I haven't heard a word she's said because *holy shit*.

I knew I was attracted to her. I mean, look at her. She's beautiful, and she's smart. Her uptight suits amuse me, and she may be the only woman on the planet who can pull them off.

But now? Now she's dressed like *that* and I know without a shadow of a doubt that I'll never be able to keep my hands off her. I have two choices. I can leave now, no harm no foul, and we both conduct our own investigations.

Or I can stay with the understanding that this isn't going to remain strictly professional for long. At least, not for me.

If she says no, well, she says no.

But damn, I hope she doesn't say no.

"Quinn?"

"Hmm?"

She frowns. "Aren't you coming inside?"

Jesus, I'm still standing in the doorway, watching her like a stupid teenager who's just got his first hard-on.

"Right." I step inside and shut the door, then turn back to find her eyes roaming up my body. I can't help but grin.

She clears her throat. "I'm, um, not used to seeing you in civilian clothes."

"Back at you," I mutter, walking to the other side of the table, and taking in the scene before me. "I brought lunch. How's it going?"

"First of all, how did you know these are my favorite sandwiches?"

"Psychic," I reply with a satisfied grin. She just rolls her eyes. She's not impressed by my usual charms, and I'll be damned if that isn't as sexy as the glasses perched on her adorable little nose.

"Second," she continues, "why did my great-grandfather save three *years'* worth of newspapers? And for the love of God, why did everyone else hang on to them after him? I had to open every single one, just to make sure that nothing important was tucked inside."

"Maybe he was saving them for a project. Or to build fires? Put on the floor when he was painting?"

She props her hand on her hip and tilts her head to the side. A strand of hair falls over her face, and she blows it out of the way.

I sit before she can see the bulge in my cargo shorts.

"Were you at the office this morning?" she asks as I open a box to get started sifting through papers.

"For a while, and then I had a movie date."

She stills, and I glance up to see her cheeks flush. She stiffens and raises her chin.

God, she's beautiful.

"You didn't have to cut a date short to come here, Quinn. I'm perfectly capable of—"

"With my niece."

Her shoulders sag, but she keeps that poker face in place. I can't help but reach over to brush my fingers over her wrist.

"I wanted to come here today. I'm sorry I couldn't come last night. I was clearing my schedule for this afternoon and tomorrow."

"Oh? Do you have plans for tomorrow?"

"I'm going to the racetrack," I reply and watch as her eyes widen. She bites her lip, then reaches into her box for more paper.

"That'll be fun."

"You should go with me."

She frowns and looks up at me. "Why in the world would I do that?"

"Because it's fun."

She laughs. "Driving fast in a circle isn't fun. Besides I get carsick."

"Bullshit."

She sets her paper down and tilts her head, blowing that strand of hair out of her face again.

"No, I really do get carsick. I'm not a good passenger."

"You'll drive your own car."

"I have to *work*, Quinn."

"It'll only be half of the day. We'll be out of there by noon, and back here combing through receipts from 1944 by two."

Her lips twitch, and I know she wants to say yes. I reach over and tuck that piece of silky hair behind her ear.

"Say yes."

"I shouldn't."

I grin, knowing that I've won this fight.

"Okay, fine, I'll go with you. But we *have* to come back here to work after. That's the deal."

"I can live with that."

She narrows her eyes on me and then goes back to looking at the papers. Suddenly, she drops everything and stands, staring at the sheet in her hand.

"Quinn, I've found something."

"Excellent."

I hurry around the table to read over her shoulder, and immediately call myself a fool. She smells too fucking good to be this close to her.

"Look." She holds it up so I can read it.

June 1, 1914

This is a receipt, showing that Lawrence Hendricks has repaid $5,000.00 of the $20,000.00 owed to Reginald House.

Reginald House
Lawrence Hendricks

"It's handwritten again," she says.

"I guess we just proved that the letter in my client's possession is authentic."

She takes a deep breath and rubs her lips together, then nods twice.

"I agree. But this also proves that my great-grandfather was paying it back. There have to be more written receipts."

She's most likely right. Sienna pulls a folder out of her briefcase and sets the receipt inside, then slips the folder back where she found it.

"High five," she says, holding her hand up for mine. I happily oblige, then pull her hand to my lips so I can kiss her knuckle and chuckle when she raises her brows, her ice-blue eyes cooling even more.

"Congratulations, Counselor."

"Thanks." Her voice is firm, but I see her swallow hard. "Do you kiss the hands of all your colleagues?"

"No." I let her go when she pulls away. "No, it seems it's

just a certain sexy redhead that I can't seem to stop thinking about. But if it makes you uncomfortable, I won't do it again."

"I'll let you know when I'm uncomfortable," she says primly and resumes digging. Rather than sit across from her, I pull up a seat next to her, and we spend the next hour combing through without finding anything else of significance.

"It's so odd that no one ever filed all those things together," she mutters. "I mean, my family isn't known for being unorganized. Except for Lou, she's as unorganized as they come."

"She sounds like the opposite of you."

"Oh, she is," she agrees with a smile. "We drive each other nuts, but we're best friends too."

"Have you talked since your fight?" I ask.

"No." She finishes her sandwich and takes her wrapper to the kitchen to toss it away, then pulls two bottles of water out of the fridge and brings me one. "I'll talk to her. We don't stay mad for long."

She sits back down and then sighs when she uncovers the next paper.

"Oh, Gramps." It's a whisper.

"What is it?"

"This is my grandparents' marriage certificate," she says, brushing her fingertips over their names. "I knew I'd come across things like this; I just wasn't expecting it to punch me in the heart. They were married for more than fifty years when she passed away."

"That's a long time."

"And they adored each other. He died less than a year after her, and I'm pretty sure he just didn't have it in him to live without her."

She wipes a tear from her cheek and tucks the marriage license in its folder, setting it aside in a pile she's started for important documents.

"I'm sorry, Sienna," I say and cover her hand with mine.

"Grief is a sneaky bitch," she mutters, and I pull her into my arms, hugging her tightly.

"You're not wrong about that." I kiss her forehead and breathe her in, just as she pulls away and wipes the last tear from her cheek.

"Sorry about that. It wasn't exactly professional."

"Neither are short-shorts and bare feet, but that's not stopping us."

She whips her gaze to mine in surprise, then dissolves into laughter. "I'm not at the office, and I didn't know for sure if you'd show. I wanted to be comfortable."

"I'm not complaining." I tuck that stray hair behind her ear again. "And when I say I'll show, I'll show. Last night wasn't planned."

"At least you texted to let me know you couldn't make it," she says with a shrug. "I didn't mind eating your tacos."

"Wait. You had tacos?"

"Yeah, I made them and everything. Brought them here. They were delicious."

"I'm sorry, Sienna."

"Like I said, not a hardship to eat your share."

"Can we have tacos tomorrow?"

She grins. "If you beat me on the track, I'll make you tacos."

"Tacos it is then."

"But if I beat you—"

I scoff, and she raises a brow.

"If I beat you, we have pizza."

"You're not going to beat me, sweetheart."

"Don't bet your law practice on it."

"You've raced before," I say for the eleventh time the following afternoon as I take a bite of my pepperoni pizza.

"Nope." She smiles smugly and takes a bite of her own slice. "I've never driven that fast. I honestly didn't think I had it in me."

"Well, you clearly do." My voice is dry, and I can't take my eyes off her. That messy bun is back today, a red tee, and cropped jeans. We're sitting at her grandfather's table, the pizza set in the middle, and I'm still buzzing with adrenaline.

I want to pull her in my lap and fuck her until we're both blind.

Instead, I take another bite of pizza.

"I think this is the first and last race for me," she admits.

"It was exhilarating, and I understand why you love it, but I'm not a thrill seeker, Quinn."

"You were excellent. Why wouldn't you want to do it again?"

"Like I said, I'm not a thrill seeker. Not an adrenaline junkie. I was scared shitless."

"But you still drove like a pro and you *beat me*. That doesn't happen every day."

"Yeah, well, I'm a little competitive. And I was *really* hungry for pizza."

I stare at her. "All this was for a pizza?"

She giggles. "And bragging rights. I outraced you today, and no one can ever take that away from me. Plus, I drove a Porsche and that's my dream car."

Her eyes widen and she stuffs more pizza in her mouth, as if she didn't mean to say that.

"It is?"

She just shrugs.

"Why didn't you say something when you were riding in my car?"

She shrugs that shoulder again, chewing. "It's silly."

"No, it isn't." I make a mental note to let her drive my car. "You're a good driver."

"I'm an *excellent* driver," she says with a happy smile. "And I'm okay with driving the speed limit and staying safe. Really. I'm the responsible one, remember?"

My phone pings with a text.

"This is London," I murmur.

> Hey! Your tickets are all set for Friday night. I got two for you, so bring a date!

"Who's in London?" she asks, licking sauce off her finger, and sending my already revved libido into overdrive.

"No one, London is the name of Finn's soon-to-be fiancée. He's going to propose next weekend."

"That's sweet."

"You might have heard of her. London Watson?"

"The actress?"

"That's her." I nod and tuck my phone away. "She's backing a new show that opens on Friday night, and she was just letting me know that my seats are saved."

My eyes narrow, an idea forming.

"Sienna, what are you doing Friday night?"

"Working." She pops the last of her crust in her mouth and carries her paper plate to the recycle bin, then washes her hands.

"Come with me, to the show."

She shakes her head. "Why me? Don't you have a harem of women just waiting for you to call?"

My lips twitch. "No. Besides, you're the only woman I've been spending any significant time with, and I'd like to take you."

"I can't keep taking time away from this case," she begins and walks around the table, away from me. "We went racing today, and that was fun, but you said yourself that these thirty days will go faster than we think, and I need to focus."

"Taking *one* evening to go to a Broadway show isn't going to kill this case," I counter. "Look at us."

I sweep my arms out, gesturing at the stacks of boxes and files.

"We're buried. I can barely see the top of your head half the time. Sienna, by Friday evening, we'll need some fresh air and a little downtime away from the paper matrix."

She smirks, and I can tell that she is considering it. Then, the smile is gone and she looks at me with serious blue eyes.

"What are we doing here, Quinn?"

"Arguing," I reply, making her laugh and shake her head.

"No. We're supposed to be keeping this professional. We have a job to do, and that's it. I don't want to jeopardize this case, it's too important."

"That's not what we're doing." I stand and walk around the table to her, take her hands in mine, and rest them against my chest. "The case is moving along, and it's safe. We both have the best interest of the case in mind. But Sienna, can you honestly say that you don't feel anything when we're together?"

Her eyes are on my lips. Her mouth opens, then closes, as if she can't get the words in her brain to form.

"I feel it," she whispers finally. "And I'm fighting it."

"Why?"

"Because it's not a good idea." She licks her lips. "Because you're opposing counsel, and I won't be the latest woman that you play with. We hadn't met before, but that doesn't mean that your reputation didn't precede you."

"Rumors aren't truth."

"Are you denying that you're a player?"

I'm a lot of things, but I'm not a liar. "I've enjoyed women. I admit that. But—"

"If you say I'm different from the rest, I'll knee you in the balls."

"I don't think I can win in this situation."

"Tell me this: Would you still ask me to go to the show with you if the chemistry wasn't here?"

"Of course not, and that's not because I'm an asshole. Which I can be. I won't apologize for being attracted to you, Sienna, and I won't make excuses for why I want to see you. Do I want to get you naked? More than I want to breathe."

She gasps, but I keep talking.

"More than that, and yes, it's new for me, I want to *be* with you. You make me laugh, and you're damn smart. I'm attracted to that very much. And I'd like your company on Friday night."

She bites her lip and glances away, and I can't stand it anymore. I cup her face and lower my lips to hers, needing to taste her.

She's spicy from the pizza and from her own sass. Her hands fist on my shirt at my sides, and I devour her, memorizing every inch, every sigh.

I pull my mouth away and rest my forehead against hers.

"That wasn't just me."

"No," she agrees.

"Come with me on Friday."

She takes a deep breath, and just when I think she's going to turn me down, she says, "Okay."

"You're damn challenging."

A slow smile slides over her face.

"Damn right I am."

Chapter Six

~Sienna~

Whelp, I've officially lost my damn mind.

I'm at a stoplight on my way home from Grandpa's house, staring at myself in the rearview mirror.

I look the same, but I don't *feel* the same at all.

I let Quinn Cavanaugh kiss me. And if I'm being honest, I didn't just let him, I participated with equal enthusiasm. Because he's not a good kisser.

No, he's a freaking exceptional kisser. The kind of kisser who should come with a damn warning label. He could win the kissing Olympics.

And now my lips are ruined for all of mankind.

"You're in way over your head," I scold myself in the mirror before the light turns green and I continue on my way.

I had one of the best days that I can remember in a long

time. Like I told Quinn, I'm no thrill seeker, but driving that car today was amazing.

Dangerous.

So out of character for me.

And when we were done, and he ran to me, boosted me in the air and spun me around in excitement?

Well, that might have been the best part of all. Seeing the pride in his brown eyes, and that big smile on his handsome face.

He didn't even give me a crazy guilt trip for winning, which surprised the hell out of me. The men I've been with, which have been few and far between, were not good losers. Their egos were ridiculously small, along with other body parts that I don't want to think about.

I had no illusions of grandeur today; I *knew* that Quinn would win that race. He told me that he's driven that track since he was a kid and his dad put him in driving school there when Quinn showed a tendency to drive too fast, and his father wanted him to have the tools to be safe.

However, I may be a safety girl, but I am also competitive, and when I got behind the wheel, it's like I suddenly became someone else.

I won by less than a car length.

And although he teased me a bit, and was truly flummoxed that I won, he was also gracious and excited for me.

And then he kissed me.

"Dumb," I mutter as I turn down my block. "Not only did

you kiss him, you agreed to go out on a *date* with him. You know better than that."

Before I can continue to give myself a stern lecture, I see Louise sitting on my front porch, in the glow of my porch light.

I get out of the car and walk up the sidewalk, and Lou stands, linking and unlinking her fingers nervously.

"You have a key," I remind her without saying hi. "You didn't have to sit out here in the dark."

"I can't just go inside when you're mad," she says and bites her lip. "And I'm really hoping that you're not mad anymore because I don't want to fight."

"Good because I need you."

"You do?"

I unlock the door and she follows me inside. I set my briefcase by the door, my keys in their bowl, and then walk into the kitchen for a bottle of wine.

I need a glass.

Or four.

"Wine?"

"Yes, please." Her voice is full of gratitude and relief. "And let me just say right now that I'm sorry for the other day. You're right, and I didn't want to hear it. I took everything back."

"Lou—"

"It was the right thing to do," she says, holding her hands up. "The sad thing, but the right one. I've been upset about

Grandpa, and just *everything* lately. Shopping helps. But I don't want to waste his money, and I don't want to fight with you."

"I'm proud of you." I pass her a glass of red and wrap my arm around her shoulders, then kiss her cheek. "You're right, you did the right thing."

"Yeah, but you should have seen that Chanel bag, Si. It was to *die* for."

"And you can still buy it, after you get the rest of your finances figured out and on your feet, splurge on the bag. It'll be a gift to yourself."

"I like that," she says and sips her wine. "Okay, enough about me. What's going on with you? What do you need me for?"

"Ironically, I need you to go shopping with me this week."

Her brown eyes widen with anticipation and excitement. "I was *not* expecting that, but I'm all for it. What are we shopping for?"

I tell her about Quinn's invitation to the play premiere.

"I don't have anything to wear."

"No, you don't." I narrow my eyes at her, and she just laughs. "I've been through your closet, and you don't have anything appropriate for an opening. But I'm happy to help you shop. When should we go?"

"I'll have to check my schedule, but we have to go soon in case I need alterations."

"This will be fun," she says and sips her wine again. "Quinn is sexy, but is he nice?"

"So far, yes."

"Marry him, because sexy and nice are hard to find."

WELL, AS SOON as possible didn't happen. It's Wednesday evening, and Lou and I are finally shopping for my dress. I was just too busy the past few days, but Quinn had to cancel for this evening, so I called Lou and here we are at Macy's in a sea of retail heaven.

"What about this?" I hold up a simple black dress and Lou wrinkles her nose.

"I didn't realize we were going for the grandma look for this."

"This isn't a grandma dress." I sound defensive, but then I give the lace and puffy sleeves another look and hang it back on the rack with a sigh. "You're right, it's a grandma dress."

"This is beautiful," Louise says. She's holding a gray dress with a simple strapless bodice and ruffly skirt. "With your complexion, you'd rock this."

"I love that." I rush over to her and she holds it up to me.

"It's perfect."

"How much is it?"

We both look for a tag and my heart sinks at the price.

"I'm not spending twelve hundred dollars on a dress."

"It's steep, but it's so perfect for you, Si."

"I'll keep looking. I have a budget of five hundred for the whole shebang. Dress, shoes, hair, and makeup."

"You're joking, right?"

I pull a three-hundred-dollar dress off the rack and hold it up.

"I'm not that funny. This is pretty."

"Yeah, for a prison guard."

"Louise, you're not helping." I roll my eyes and set the dress aside, then move on.

"There are going to be a lot of people at this thing, Sienna, and they're going to be wearing expensive things. You can't show up in a three-hundred-dollar dress."

"Well, that's exactly what I'm doing, and if Quinn doesn't like it, he doesn't have to take me. Now, are you going to help me with this or not?"

"Of course," she says with a disappointed sigh. "Here is a simple little black dress. With the right shoes and clutch, along with jewelry, we can work with this."

"And it's only two hundred," I say with excitement. "I'll try it on. Here's hoping it fits because we don't have time for alterations."

Twenty minutes later, I'm satisfied with the fit of the dress. It flatters my long legs and isn't too low cut around the girls. I'll feel sexy but not self-conscious.

"It's a keeper," I say triumphantly. "And I can totally wear my black heels with it."

"No." Louise shakes her head adamantly. "Absolutely not. Those heels are fine for work, and I'm being kind with that statement, but they are *not* okay for this dress. You want sexy, not matronly."

"They're comfortable, they're black, and they'll match it fine."

"No. I'm not bending on this one, Sienna. We'll find something on sale."

She drags me to the giant shoe section and finds five shoes off the bat that don't break the bank and are appropriate for the occasion.

"Wow, these are on sale for fifty bucks," she says with excitement. "Try them first."

They're black, and about two inches taller than the ones I normally wear. They're not supercomfortable, but for the price, they'll do.

"Sold," I announce. "This wasn't so bad. I have some jewelry at home."

"And I can do your hair," Lou says. "It'll be like prom."

"God, I hope it's *not* like prom."

My phone pings with a text. I glance down and smile when I see Quinn's name.

> Hi Sienna. I need a favor. Do you mind coming into the city to meet at my office tomorrow night? I know it's not ideal, but I have a late meeting, and I don't want to lose another evening of work with you.

"Oh my God, he doesn't want to miss an evening with you," Lou says and shakes my arm.

"Stop reading over my shoulder."

"Not gonna happen," she says with a laugh as I type out my response.

> Not a problem. I'll bring a couple of boxes with me.
> What time should I be there?

We take the dress and the shoes to the cashier. As she's ringing up my purchases, Quinn replies.

> 7:00 would be perfect. I'll have dinner brought in.

I reply with See you then and shove my phone in my bag, pay for my purchases, and Louise and I walk out to my car.

"You're going to look fantastic," she says. What she doesn't say is *even though you were cheap and didn't spring for the pretty dress.*

But this is who I am, and if Quinn doesn't like it, well, he doesn't have to.

I PULL UP to Quinn's office building the next evening and am not surprised to hear that he's already buzzed me through security to park in the private lot, and he's arranged to have two guys come down and carry the boxes up for me.

Which is good because paper is *heavy.*

"We have these, Ms. Hendricks. Follow us," one of the young men says. They're both in suits and look young enough to be law clerks or junior attorneys.

I remember those days.

They escort me up the elevator, and rather than walk into the conference room that I'd seen the last time I was here, they lead me in the opposite direction to Quinn's office.

I'm *very* interested to see how Quinn decorated his office.

The door is open, so the guys walk ahead of me and place the boxes on a table across the room from his desk.

The room is fucking huge. You could host a party for sixty people in this room. Quinn's desk is massive and black, with two monitors, papers, pens and pencils, and folders covering half the surface. His chair is also black and large.

It looks supercomfortable.

The table where my boxes are now sitting is big enough to seat six. The boxes are on one end, and it looks like food containers are at the other.

He also has a large gray couch, two yellow chairs, all situated before a fireplace.

In contrast, my office is about the size of a cubicle and I had to rummage through a storage room to find a chair that wasn't from 1955.

"Hey," he says after the guys leave and shuts the door behind them. "Thank you for coming all this way."

"It's really not a problem," I reply with a smile. "You come out my way every day, so it's only fair that I come to you when you need me to."

He grins, and looks like he wants to say something, but there's a knock on his door, and another man walks in.

He looks like he could be Quinn's twin.

"I'm leaving," he announces, then stops when he sees me. "I don't think we've met."

"Finn, this is Sienna Hendricks. Sienna, this is my brother, Finn."

"Hi," I say with a smile and shake his outstretched hand. "It's nice to meet you."

"Likewise," he replies. Jesus, the Cavanaughs have excellent genes.

"Are you nervous?" Quinn asks Finn, who frowns and shoves his hands in his pockets.

"I'm fucking terrified," he admits, but then shrugs. "It's a new thing for me."

"Why are you terrified?" I ask, not at all shy about asking. If they didn't want me to know, they wouldn't be talking about it in front of me.

"I'm proposing to my girlfriend this weekend. After the show tomorrow night, we're headed to our place at the beach."

"That's right, Quinn mentioned it. Is that the ring?" I gesture to the blue box in his hand, and he smiles proudly.

"Yes, do you want to see it?"

"Hell yes, I want to see it."

Both men chuckle as Finn unwraps the box and opens the black box inside, revealing a pear-shaped diamond the size of a baby's fist.

Holy fucking shit. This looks like it belongs in the crown jewels.

"Well?" Finn asks. "Do you think she'll like it?"

"If she doesn't, she's not a woman," I reply when I find my voice. "This is absolutely stunning, Finn."

"Told you," Quinn says and pats his brother on the back. "She's going to lose her shit."

I think I just lost my shit.

In fact, I know I did.

That ring cost Finn more than I make in a year. I've lost sight of how different Quinn and I are while he's been coming out to the Bronx to work with me. Despite the Porsche, I've forgotten how polar opposite we are on the financial spectrum.

And I'm perfectly okay with not being wealthy.

But Louise was right, I don't fit in. My five-hundred-dollar budget for the show tomorrow night is a joke. Hell, the suit he's wearing right now had to cost four times that much, and he's just at work.

In contrast, I'm wearing a suit that I got on sale for two hundred dollars.

I'm not saying I'm less than him. I'm not.

But I don't belong here either.

"Thanks for the confidence booster," Finn says with a smile. "We'll see you tomorrow night?"

I nod, unable to admit that I've begun to consider pulling out of the date.

But Quinn is all smiles as he escorts his brother to the door, confirms that we'll be there early to see the family, and then turns to me when we're alone.

Jesus, I have to meet his family.

"I'm not going tomorrow night," I announce. My voice sounds high to my own ears, but I swallow hard and raise my chin, trying to look more confident than I am.

Quinn's eyes narrow as he pushes his hands in his pockets and walks slowly toward me.

"What just happened here?"

"I just can't go. I'm sorry to do this to you last minute." I walk over to the boxes on the table and take the lid off one, just to have something to do with my hands. "I think it's best if we keep this strictly professional."

"Too late," he says simply. I turn in surprise. He's taken his jacket off, and he's rolling his sleeves up his forearms. "And I've had a shit day, I didn't get to spend time with you last night, and now you're saying that you don't want to go to London's show with me. So I'm going to need an explanation."

"I'm sorry, Quinn, I just . . . You know—" I bite my lip and silently yell at myself to get it together. "It's the normal things. I probably need to wash my hair, and I've felt a headache coming on for a few days now. Not to mention, I promised my sister I'd bake her a cake this weekend, so I might as well just get started on that."

Louise has never asked me to bake her a cake in her life, but he doesn't know that.

"Stop."

I set the papers that I'd picked up back in the box and turn to face him. He doesn't look angry, or upset.

He looks confused.

Well, join the club, pal.

"Sienna, this is not you. What's going on here?"

"I don't belong here," I blurt out and then hate myself for it.

He frowns. "Of course you do. I asked you here."

"No. Yes, you did, but that's not what I'm talking about." I take a deep breath and let it out slowly, then square my shoulders. "Okay, I'll cut to the chase. I don't intimidate easily. But I'm intimidated. Not professionally, let me just say that right now, although I'm certain that when you designed these offices it was with the intention that it would intimidate anyone who came here for meetings.

"You did a good job of that, by the way."

"Thanks. Let's skip to the personal part."

"You and I, we're just . . . *different.*"

"So? If we were exactly the same, it would be boring. And you're not boring, Sienna."

How do I tell him that I don't want to embarrass him? Or myself? That Quinn and his expensive lifestyle are just overwhelming and I don't think I'm the right person to get mixed up in it?

"You're overthinking this," he says and steps to me. Shit, if he touches me, I'll do pretty much anything he wants me to.

So I back away, and he scowls at that.

"I don't ever want you to back away from me like that. I would never hurt you."

"I'm not afraid of you," I reply. *Much.* "But if you touch

me, I'll agree to whatever you propose, and I've made my decision."

"Because you think you don't belong here, whatever that means."

He rubs his hand over his face in frustration.

"We're in different leagues," I reply. "You're chrome and glass and a Porsche, and I'm old offices and a Ford."

"Fuck that." His eyes are angry now, and he steps to me, not touching me, but close enough that I can smell him. "You don't get to label me based on my office or the car I drive, Sienna, any more than I get to label *you* for those things. I don't come from money, and I don't give a fuck about what your office looks like. I enjoy you. I want to spend an evening with you, and my family. It's that basic. If you don't want to go, just say so, but don't make up some chickenshit excuse about cakes and headaches, and don't ever throw my money in my face. I work damn hard for what I have, just like you do."

Well, shit.

Now I feel embarrassed and ashamed.

I should.

Quinn stalks away from me and stares out of his office window to the city. The sun is setting, and the buildings are lit up.

"I refuse to apologize for my success," he mutters.

I press my fingers into my eyes, and then I take a deep breath and prepare myself for the apology that he deserves.

"I fucked up."

"Big-time," he agrees.

I cross to him, and stand next to him, crossing my arms over my chest and staring out the window.

"I bought a dress yesterday," I begin.

"For a date that you don't want to go on?"

I blow out a breath and shake my head. "No, for a date I *do* want to go on. But it's not an expensive dress, Quinn. Because I'm just a simple girl. It's pretty, though."

"I don't give a rat's ass how much your dress cost," he says softly. "You'd be beautiful in a burlap sack."

"It takes a special kind of girl to pull off burlap," I say, trying to lighten the mood. I glance up to find his lips twitching. "I'm sorry for being dumb."

Without looking at me, he drapes his arm around my shoulders and tugs me into his side.

"You're not dumb."

"I'm also not usually insecure."

"Good." He presses his lips onto the top of my head and breathes in deeply. "Because it's not sexy."

"Well, we can't have that, can we?"

"Come on, let's eat this food before it's cold and get started on work. I don't think you're ready for the alternative scenario I have running through my head."

I swallow in surprise, and he chuckles next to me.

"Don't worry, sweetheart. We aren't there yet."

"Work it is, then."

Chapter Seven

~Sienna~

$\mathcal{I}$ hope you're hungry," Quinn says as we drive into Manhattan Friday evening. It's early, giving us plenty of time to linger over dinner before we head to the show.

"I think I've proven over the past week or so that I have a healthy appetite," I reply with a laugh. The evening is off to a great start. He looks amazing in his dark gray suit and red tie, which just happens to match my red clutch and ruby earrings.

"I like a girl who isn't afraid to eat," he replies. "And this restaurant is delicious."

"What kind of food is it?"

"Italian."

"Excellent." I rub my hands together in anticipation. I *am* hungry. And I'm so happy that I didn't give in to my ridiculous insecurities and cheat myself out of tonight because I'm already having a great time.

Quinn finds parking near Fifth Avenue, opens my door for me, and takes my hand as he leads me down the sidewalk.

"We're going to Armani," he says.

"Do you need to shop?"

He grins. "No, they have an excellent restaurant."

"Really? I hadn't heard. This will be fun."

Just then, my heel gets stuck in one of the sidewalk grates, and the next split second happens in slow motion.

I feel the heel pop off my shoe, and I lose my balance, falling forward and scraping up my hand.

"Shit, Sienna, are you okay?"

Humiliated but I'm going to live.

"I'm okay." I work my broken heel out of the grate and feel my heart sink. "I guess this is what I get when I buy cheap shoes."

"No, this is what you get when your date doesn't steer you away from the damn grate."

I smile up at Quinn as he helps me to my feet. People are bustling by, but I'm not paying attention to them.

I'm too mortified.

"I can fix this," I say. "Is there a CVS Pharmacy nearby where I can get some superglue? Chewing gum? Hell, I could probably make a Band-Aid work."

"This isn't DIY, Sienna," Quinn replies with a frown. "We'll get you some shoes."

I sigh, my cheeks hot and I'm sure I'm bright red. "There *is* plenty of shopping here, but do we have time?"

"Lots of time," he assures me. "And there's Bergdorf's right here."

"I'm more of a Macy's kind of girl."

"There's no time for that," he replies, helping me hobble across the street with one good heel and one broken one. I'm walking like the hunchback of Notre Dame.

"I'm going to slip into the restroom real quick," I say when we've walked inside the store. "I need to wash my hands."

"Of course. I'll wait for you here."

I nod, walk into the restroom, and lean on the vanity, taking a deep breath.

"Jesus, wouldn't it just figure that I'd manage to fall on my face in Manhattan with the sexiest man alive?"

I shake my head as I wash my sore hands and check myself everywhere else to make sure I'm not bleeding or bruised, but it looks like it's just my hands, shoe, and pride that are hurt.

"I can splurge on a pair of shoes," I assure my reflection. "I told Lou just the other day to buy herself the Chanel bag as a treat to herself, and I can do the same for the shoes. I'll wear them for work as well, so it won't be a wasted splurge."

Once I'm cleaned up and have talked myself into spending the money on some designer shoes, I join Quinn, who escorts me up the elevator to the shoe department.

I've always loved shoes. And now that the idea is in my head, I'm kind of excited to pick out something extra beautiful.

And, let's get real, if I'm going to splurge, I'm going to *splurge.* So I head straight for the Louboutin section.

"Good taste," Quinn mutters with a smile as I begin to touch the toes of beautiful shoes, in all heel sizes.

But then I see them. Black heels in patent leather with that signature red sole, and I know I'm a goner.

"I'll try these in a thirty-nine, please," I say to the salesman, Roger, who hasn't been far away.

"Of course," he says with a slight bow and hurries off to the stockroom.

I slip out of the broken shoes, with the intention to ask Roger to toss them away. They're ruined.

"It smells good in here," I say with a smile and Quinn grins.

"Are you a shoe girl?"

"Of course, I'm female." I laugh and fiddle with my grandmother's ruby necklace. "I've always wanted a pair of these, and this is an excellent excuse to get them."

Roger returns, and I slide my feet into the heels, delighted that they fit perfectly. I walk around the couches, to make sure they don't slip off my heels, but they don't.

They feel like heaven.

"I'll take them," I inform the happy Roger and reach for my clutch. When I pull out my credit card, Roger shakes his head.

"No, miss, these have already been taken care of."

My gaze whips to Quinn, who just shrugs, his eyes wide and innocent.

He's so not innocent.

"I don't know," he says and shakes his head. I'm not going to argue here, that would be rude. So I keep my new shoes on, ask Roger to toss the old ones, and soon we're walking back toward Armani, only a few minutes late for our reservation.

"You didn't have to buy me shoes," I say as I slip my hand in his.

"I don't do much in life that I don't want to do, Sienna." He lifts my hand to his lips and kisses my knuckles. "Your legs are fucking amazing in these heels. But if it truly bothers you, consider it payment for the painting."

"Thank you."

"You're welcome."

DESPITE THE SHOE debacle, dinner was delicious and intimate, and we arrive at the show with plenty of time to see Quinn's family before it starts.

"Hello, dear, I'm Quinn's mother, Maggie."

"Hello, Mrs. Cavanaugh."

"Please, call me Maggie," she says with a friendly smile. "Everyone does. You're simply lovely this evening."

"Oh, thank you very much."

Quinn introduces me to Carter, and his daughter, Gabby. Finn joins us, smiling widely.

"London will join us just after she's finished saying hello to everyone backstage," he says. "She's so damn excited."

"As she should be," Maggie replies and pats her son on the shoulder. "We're all very proud of her."

"I really like your shoes," Gabby says to me with a smile.

She's a beautiful girl, with dark hair and blue eyes. She's in a pretty red dress and black shoes.

"Thank you."

"I asked Daddy for some for Christmas, but he said no."

"You're too young for designer shoes," Carter says and sighs. "Ask me again when you're thirty."

"Daddy." She rolls her eyes and then laughs. "He still likes to think I'm a baby."

"You'll always be my baby," Carter says as we all find our seats. We have a whole box to ourselves, with an excellent view of the stage.

"Gabby, how would you like to go with me to Hawaii again this summer?" Maggie asks her granddaughter, who immediately grins and claps her hands.

"Yessss!"

"Maggie, you don't have to—" Carter begins, but Maggie shakes her head.

"She's my only granddaughter, thanks to these bozos taking their sweet time, and I want to spend some time alone with her."

"Awesome," Gabby says. "I want to snorkel again."

"Mom, do you think it's a good idea to travel right now?" Quinn asks her, and she turns to him, pinning him in a glare.

"Quinn, I'm a grown woman, who can travel whenever she pleases."

"Yes, ma'am," Quinn says, but I can tell that the subject isn't over.

"Hi, everyone." London joins us, her face flushed with excitement. She's beautiful in a white dress with diamonds sparkling at her ears and her neck.

I can't wait to hear how the proposal goes.

"London, I'd like for you to meet Sienna," Quinn says, and London immediately pulls me in for a hug.

"Welcome," she says with a smile. "It's so nice to meet you."

"Same here. Congratulations on tonight, and all your recent success."

"Thank you," she replies with a big smile. "It's a big night."

"We're just thrilled for you, London," Carter says, and the lights blink on and off, signaling that it's time for the show to start.

Everyone sits, the whole auditorium a buzz of excitement for the show. It's been critically acclaimed already.

It's heavy. Important. About addiction and love. Family. Hurts and healing.

I find myself wiping tears from my cheeks, and Quinn passes me a handkerchief. A real one.

I had no idea that men still carried these.

But I accept it and dab carefully at my eyes, trying to salvage my makeup. He takes my hand in his and links our fingers together, holding on tightly.

God, I love the way it feels when he touches me. He's warm and strong. Solid.

Safe.

Is that weird? I've known the man for such a short time, and yet, I feel completely at ease with him.

Quinn leans in, presses his lips to my ear, and whispers, "You're so damn beautiful. I can't wait to get you home."

And just like that, I forget about how little I know him, how we're working a case together and that we're sitting among all his family.

I want him. I *like* him. And this is new territory for me, but I've decided that I won't overthink it to death.

I'm going to enjoy him.

"IT WAS STUNNING," I assure London an hour later as I offer her a hug. "I loved it. You should be very proud."

"I'm *so* proud," she says with a watery grin. "I'm so happy that you came. I'd love to get together for lunch sometime."

"I'd like that," I reply with a nod. "I'll have Quinn send you my number."

"Perfect. I'll text you. Would you all like to come backstage?"

"We will pass," Quinn says before I can reply, and I'm relieved. I'm ready to be alone with him. "But thank you for the invitation. Sienna's right, it was fabulous."

We say our good-byes to his family, and then leave, walking hand in hand to his car.

"Your family is really nice."

He nods and smiles softly down at me. "They liked you."

"I liked them too. But you sound surprised. Are you surprised that they liked me?"

"No." He laughs and opens the car door for me, then walks around and joins me. "You're a likable woman, of course they like you."

"They're all very nice. London is beautiful. I hope the proposal goes well."

"Finn will be just fine," Quinn says. "Sienna, I'd like to take you home."

I frown. "I thought that's where we were headed."

"No, I mean to *my* home. I'd like to show you my condo."

"Oh, that sounds nice. I'd like to see where you live." I knew it was going to lead to this. I *knew*. But I didn't expect to be so nervous. Butterflies are doing the cha-cha in my belly, but I'm excited too. I can't wait to see his place.

"Excellent."

He drives through Manhattan, and it doesn't take us long to reach his building. He parks underground, then escorts me to an elevator that takes us up to the penthouse level. The doors open, and we step out of the elevator, but I'm struck speechless.

I'm not sure if I've ever seen a more beautiful space in my life. I expected Quinn's space to be modern. Sleek. Simple.

But it's opulent and lovely. Full of color. Plush furniture and polished oak floors that my shoes click on as I walk through the space.

Quinn is taking his jacket off and rolling his sleeves, the

way he always does when it's time to get comfortable. I set my clutch on a table and continue to wander, taking everything in.

It's an open floor plan, and the kitchen is ridiculously big, with everything even the most celebrated chef could need.

But it's the fireplace, and the framed painting mounted above it, that catches my eye.

"My painting," I murmur as I walk toward it, then cross my arms over my chest and stare up at it. He used reclaimed wood to frame it.

"It's my favorite piece," he says behind me. His hands rest on my shoulders, and I feel his touch throughout my whole body. My nipples pucker. My core tightens.

This man is potent.

"It's like it was made for this spot," I reply as he holds a snifter full of amber whiskey in front of me. I take the glass and sip, feeling the burn of the liquor all the way to my belly. "Thank you."

"Sienna," he begins and turns me to face him. "If you're not interested in being intimate with me tonight, I need to take you home right now."

"I'm not going home," I reply immediately. My voice is strong and sure, just as strong as my conviction to stay.

I want him, and I won't apologize for it.

His eyes are pinned to mine as he swallows the rest of his drink and sets the glass aside. I take a final sip and pass my glass to him, and he sets it next to his.

"Shall I show you the rest of my place?"

So he's not going to attack me right here in his living room. Good. There's no hurry.

I bite my lip and nod, and he slips his hand in mine and leads me down a hallway.

"How long have you lived here?" I ask.

"Three years," he replies. "I hated it when I bought it. Everything was white. I mean, *everything*. The walls, the floors, the furniture. Even the appliances."

"That's a lot of white. They must not have had kids."

He laughs and opens a door, flips on a light, and I'm in his home office. It's a good size, with big windows. Like the man who owns it, the furniture is big and imposing. A bit intimidating.

Sexy.

"So I bought it, and before I moved in I hired a decorator and told her what I wanted. She did well."

"I like it," I agree with a nod. "Sounds like when I bought my place."

"I remember," he says, his lips twitching. "We have a lot in common."

He leads me farther down the hall and points out a guest bath, a guest bedroom, and at the end of the hall, he opens double doors to reveal the master suite.

"It's softer in here," I murmur, dropping his hand so I can run my fingers over the soft bedding. The colors are muted grays and white. It's still masculine, but much more soothing than the rest of the house.

"Wait until you see the bathroom," he says with a satisfied grin. I walk through a massive walk-in closet that would give most women wet dreams and gasp at the threshold of the bathroom.

"Jesus," I whisper. The tub is big enough for a party of four, freestanding against a wall of windows that look out onto the city. "I hope these are privacy windows."

"Of course." He's leaning his shoulder on the doorjamb, watching me with a half smile on his lips. "I'm not an exhibitionist."

"Good to know."

There's an empty vanity table with a pretty gray velvet chair. It would be a great place to get ready for work or a night out.

The cabinetry and countertops are as opulent as the rest of the condo, and once again I'm reminded of just how different Quinn and I are.

But the insecurity doesn't fill me the way it did the other night. Instead, I feel proud of him. He was right, he *does* work hard, and he shouldn't ever have to apologize for having nice things.

"This is a beautiful room," I murmur, then turn to find that his eyes have turned from lazy and happy to fierce and full of lust. "What?"

"When you bite your lip like that, it makes *me* want to bite it."

I feel my brows climb, and I tilt my head to the side, watching him. His hands are in his pockets, as usual. I love how the muscles in his forearms flex, as if he's fisting and unfisting his hands with agitation.

"You say what's on your mind, don't you?"

"I'm not one for bullshit."

And that's why I'm so attracted to him. Aside from the fact that the man has a body that should come with a warning label, I like that he speaks his mind, and that I don't have to guess what he's thinking.

And by the way he's looking at me right now, I'd say he wants me naked.

Usually being the one to let the man take the lead, I don't know that I've ever been this bold in my life, but Quinn gives me confidence. He makes me feel beautiful. Powerful.

It's as intoxicating as the liquor he served me when we first arrived.

With my eyes pinned to his, I reach behind me and lower the zipper of my simple black dress. Thank God it's easy to get in and out of. As soon as the zipper is lowered, it falls in a billowy heap around my feet, and I'm standing before him in a strapless black bra, tiny black lacy panties, and a smile.

He swallows hard. Twice.

Then he pushes away from the doorway and reaches out for my hand, which I take and step out of the dress.

"You're going to keep those shoes on," he murmurs as he leans in and presses his lips to mine. "Everything else goes."

Before I can reply, he sweeps me up in his arms and walks into the bedroom, where the light beside the bed is low, and we can see the city glow through another wall of windows.

"More privacy glass," he assures me before kissing me tenderly just above my collarbone. He's still holding me as he pulls the covers back, then lays me down in the middle of the bed, leaving me in my underwear and shoes so he can shuck out of his own clothes.

The light flickers over his body, and I lean up on my elbows to take in the show. Holy shit. He's all smooth, bronze skin and lean muscle. He has a light spattering of hair on his chest, and a happy trail that leads down to, well, a treasure.

I immediately reach out for his cock, but he intercepts my hand, kisses it, and climbs over me, kissing his way up my torso.

"If you touch me now," he says between peppering kisses over my stomach, "I'll lose my control, and that would be embarrassing."

"So, you get to touch me, but I don't get to touch you?" My breath catches when he tugs my bra down and he traces the edge of my nipple with the tip of his tongue.

"Correct."

"I object."

He smiles up at me and hooks my panties in his thumbs, pulling them down my legs.

"Overruled," he replies. He buries his nose in my panties, takes a deep breath, then tosses them over his shoulder and spreads me wide.

Holy fuck.

"Jesus, you're beautiful," he whispers as his thumbs glide up through my already wet folds. He circles my clit, then his fingers move down and plunge inside me as he nibbles on the inside of my thigh.

"Oh, God," I moan, my hips circling. He hitches my leg over his shoulder, and I have to admit, it looks damn sexy with that shoe. "The shoes were a good call."

"I know."

And with that, his mouth descends on my core, and he takes me for the ride of my life. The world explodes around me, and before it falls back together again, Quinn climbs over me, kissing his way up my body, and his cock is resting against me.

"Condom," I say.

"It's on," he assures me with a grin. "You were too busy coming to notice."

All I can do is grin as he slips inside me, and then I sigh as he moves, in and out, over again, chasing both of our orgasms.

I bear down, my spine tingling, and am surprised with a second orgasm so quickly. Quinn buries his face in my neck and cries out as he comes, his body slick with sweat and hard everywhere.

"I've changed my mind," I mutter and swallow around my dry mouth.

"Too late," he replies, panting.

"Not about that." I laugh as he rolls to the side and kisses the ball of my shoulder. "I think I've decided that I'm a thrill seeker after all, if this is what it gets me."

"Damn right it does."

Chapter Eight

~Quinn~

I should go."

Sienna sits up, my sheet wrapped around her delectable little body, and makes a move to walk into the bathroom, but I snag her around the waist and haul her back onto the bed, making her giggle.

I love the sound of her laugh.

"Why?" I ask, brushing her strawberry-blond hair off her cheek, then press a kiss there. "I think you should stay."

And those are five words I've never said to another woman a day in my life. I'm usually ready for them to leave. Not because I'm an asshole, but because I'd rather not actually sleep with anyone.

But Sienna's different, and the thought of her leaving now, well, it's not an option.

She wrinkles her nose. "I have literally *nothing* here, Quinn. No clothes."

"Don't need them."

"No toothbrush."

"I have a brand-new one you can have."

"And I probably shouldn't take the walk of shame out of your condo in the morning."

Okay, that one pisses me off.

"Number one," I begin, tugging the sheet loose around her so I can let my hand roam over her soft skin. "There's no shame in what we did, or what we will do. We're consenting adults, and what we do is our business."

"It's a figure of speech—"

"Two," I interrupt, "you can have my things."

"What things?"

I jump off the bed and disappear into the closet, then return with my boxers and a T-shirt. "See? Now you have things."

She bites her lip, her blue eyes lit with humor and lust.

"So you're saying I should stay."

I laugh, toss my clothes on a nearby chair, and return to the bed and Sienna. I can't seem to stop kissing her. My hand travels down her stomach, headed to home base, when she clutches my wrist, stopping my progression.

"If you're expecting round two, you're going to have to feed me. Orgasms make me hungry."

I kiss her soundly, then climb from the bed, motivated to give her sustenance. Once we've both pulled on some clothes, we walk out to my kitchen. I turn the lights on low and take stock of the fridge.

"So it's looking like a ham-and-cheese sandwich," I mutter before looking over my shoulder at her, where she's sitting at the breakfast bar. "Or takeout."

"The sandwich sounds great," she says happily, swiveling back and forth on the stool.

"It's not fancy."

"After-sex snacks aren't supposed to be fancy," she replies with a laugh. "I'll happily eat the sandwich."

"Oh, I have Doritos too." I walk into the pantry and return with a big red bag of chips, pass them to her, then get to work building our sandwiches.

"Perfect." She munches away, watching me slice tomato for the sandwich. "And you lied. That's a fancy sandwich."

"I'm not just going to slap a slice of ham between two pieces of bread and hand it to you," I reply dryly. "I want you to actually come back here."

"Well, good sex and Doritos is a good way to lure me in." She chuckles and takes another bite of a chip. "So is this normal for you?"

"Nothing with you is normal," I say, making her tilt her head to the side the way she does when she's trying to figure something out. "And I mean that in a good way."

"Proceed," she says, as if she's drilling a witness, and my dick twitches. Jesus, I love the way her voice sounds in the courtroom.

"Well, I don't make a habit of bringing women home."

"Yeah, I could see why you're embarrassed by this place," she says with a nod, trying to look serious, but her lips are twitching.

"You're sassy tonight."

"Every night."

I close her sandwich, cut it in half, and pass it to her. She takes a big bite and sighs in happiness, which only makes my dick harder.

"Okay, this is a *really* good sandwich. Now, you were saying?"

"If I bring a woman here, she doesn't stay the night."

"I told you I'm happy to go home."

"Until you."

This makes her stop chewing and stare at me with a frown, then she swallows her bite and reaches for a Dorito.

"Why?"

"Why you?"

She nods.

"I enjoy you," I begin as I close my own sandwich and take a bite, thinking about it as I chew. "But it's more than that. I've started to *crave* my time with you, and when it's interrupted, I'm pissed."

"Well, that's not a horrible thing to hear."

"It puts me in a vulnerable position, and that's not something I'm used to, Sienna."

"Me either."

I take a bite, watching her.

"I like your confidence. Your honesty. And your legs are fucking gold."

She grins, walks her empty plate around the island to place in the sink, then looks at her fingers.

Without missing a beat, she drags her fingers, covered in Dorito cheese, down my cheek.

"Did you just do that?"

"They were dirty."

I finish my sandwich, then haul her over my shoulder, stomping to the bathroom.

"Hey! Where are we going?"

"We need a shower."

"I just need to wash my hands." She giggles, slapping my ass.

"I need to fuck you in my shower," I reply, and she stills.

"Carry on, then."

"I'M SO DISGUSTED," Sienna says the next day as we're sitting in her grandfather's dining room, sifting through more boxes.

"What's up?"

"I'm just so disappointed in my family's filing skills, or the lack thereof," she says with a sigh and leans back in her chair, stretching her arms over her head. We swung by her place on our way over today so she could change into her own clothes. She chose a tight black T-shirt and cutoff denim shorts.

And now that I know what she looks like naked, well, that's pretty much all I see when I look at her.

"I mean, I'm meticulous in how I file at the office *and* at home," she continues as she stands and walks into the kitchen for a bottle of water. "It's like my grandfather just randomly chucked papers into boxes as he was moving out of his office."

"Maybe it wasn't him," I suggest. "He might have hired movers to do it. They don't care about order."

"True." She returns to the table and sits, pulling another stack of papers over to look through. "But it makes the OCD in me twitchy."

"I get it." I chuckle and my phone rings. "It's Finn. Hey, what's up?"

"She said yes," he says, his voice full of excitement.

"Of course she did," I reply with a laugh. "The Cavanaugh men are quite a catch."

Sienna rolls her eyes, and I raise a brow, making her giggle.

"I just wanted to call and give you the official news. And you and Carter were right. Proposing here was absolutely the right thing. It was meaningful and intimate."

"Did you cry?" I demand.

"No, but she did." I can hear the satisfaction in his voice, and it makes me happy for him. "She's already talking about dates and venues."

"Well, congratulations, big brother. I'm happy for you."

"Congratulations from me too," Sienna calls out.

"Tell her thanks. I really like her, Quinn."

"Me too. Have fun, and I'll see you in a few days."

I hang up and set my phone aside.

"She said yes."

"I hope so, since I congratulated him," she says with a laugh. "That's exciting. How long have they been together?"

"About a year," I reply. "But we knew not long after they started dating that London was the one for Finn. She had him tied in knots. It was fun to watch."

"I wish Louise would find a nice guy," she says. "She always chooses guys who don't have their shit together, you know? I don't know how many times she's started dating someone, and the next thing I know she's loaning them money, or they're staying at her place."

"And what do you attract?" I ask her.

"No one."

"That's bullshit, Sienna."

"No, it's not. I work, I paint, and I spend a lot of time with my family. I haven't had much time to date."

I want to keep asking her questions about her past, yet at the same time, I don't. I'm not a jealous man, but the thought of her fucking someone else fills me with rage, so it's probably best to drop the subject.

Just as I'm about to ask her what she'd like for lunch, she jumps out of her chair and thrusts her fist in the air.

"Yes! I knew it!"

"What did you find?"

"Another receipt for five thousand dollars. See? He paid it back, Quinn."

I take the letter from her and read it, nodding.

"At least half of it, anyway."

"Oh, come on. We both know he paid it all back, we just have to find the other receipts." She pushes her glasses on her face and reaches for another stack of papers with renewed energy.

I don't mention that we don't have proof that the rest of the money was paid back, but we're off to a good start. It's not good news for my client, who's anxious to get his hands on that property.

At the end of the day, I get paid the same, whether my client is the rightful owner or not.

"Ew." She makes a face and holds a piece of paper up between her finger and thumb. "I think there's a dead roach on this."

"What is it?"

"A memo that has nothing to do with our case."

"Just throw it away then."

She stares at me like I just suggested she burn the house down.

"I can't throw anything away."

"It has a dead roach on it, Sienna. Throw it away."

She frowns and takes the paper into the kitchen to toss it, just as my phone rings again.

"Hey, Gabs."

"Uncle Quinn." She's crying, and my whole body is instantly on high alert. "I think you should come to Grandma's house."

"What's going on, baby?"

"I tried to call Daddy, but he didn't answer."

"It's okay, what's wrong? Is Grandma okay?"

Sienna's already grabbing her purse and keys, watching me with wide blue eyes.

"She's not hurt," Gabby says, sniffling. "But she's acting weird. She keeps calling me Darcy. Why does she think I'm Mom?"

I rub my hand down my face. "I don't know, baby. It's just a mistake. You do look a lot like your mama."

"No, she's confused when I tell her she said the wrong name. It's scaring me."

"Okay, I'm on my way over right now. It'll take about a half hour for me to get there. Are you okay?"

"Yeah, she's watching TV now and I went to my room."

"I'll be there very soon, Gabs. Don't worry."

I hang up and Sienna's ready to leave with me, which makes me pause.

"You don't have to come with me."

"Uh, yeah I do. I'm not going to let you go alone. You're worried, and if you need something, I'll be with you."

I frown, but before I can say anything, she takes my hand in hers.

"Hey, let's go. It's going to be okay."

I nod and lead her out to my car and hurry toward my mom's place.

"She's been acting weird lately," I say as I shift gears and change lanes. "Last week, she called me Finn. She said my father had called, and he's been dead for five years."

Sienna lays her hand on my thigh. "Take a deep breath, Quinn. Seriously, you can't do anyone any good if we don't get there in one piece."

I look down at the speedometer and cringe, easing off the gas. "Sorry, it's a habit."

"It's okay. There has to be an explanation for your mom's confusion."

"Alzheimer's," I reply grimly.

"You don't know that. It could be a lot of things."

"One thing I do know is, she shouldn't be taking Gabby to Hawaii on her own. No way."

"Let's deal with what's happening today before you take on the next month of activities. I'm not saying this isn't serious, because it certainly is, but there could be several explanations."

I nod and take a deep breath. I feel better having Sienna with me. I would normally have already called an ambulance to come get her, and my anxiety would be through the roof. I *am* worried, but I'm not freaking out.

"Thanks for coming with me."

"Of course."

We make it to Mom's house in twenty-five minutes. We walk inside without knocking, and I find Mom watching TV in the living room, with Gabby sitting at the kitchen table, looking at her phone.

"What are you doing here?" Mom asks.

"Well, we thought we'd come by because Gabby called and

said you were a little confused today," I reply as I sit next to Mom. She frowns and glances over at Gabby.

"I'm not confused, Darcy."

Sienna and I exchange looks, and Gabby immediately breaks down in tears.

"Gabby, why don't you and I go into the kitchen and let Quinn and your grandmother talk?"

Gabby leads Sienna out of the room, and I turn the TV off, getting Mom's attention.

"What in the world is everyone fretting over?"

"You called her Darcy," I reply and take Mom's hand in mine. "It upset her, Mom."

"I'm sure I didn't do that, Finn."

"Quinn."

She frowns at me.

"That's what I said."

"No, you called me Finn. Mom, this confusion is getting worse, and I think you should see your doctor about it. Monday."

"I have an appointment on Monday," she says with a sigh. "I'll tell him about it."

"Do you want me to go with you?"

"No, because you make a big deal out of nothing at all, and I'm a grown woman. I can go to the doctor without a chaperone."

"This is serious, Mom. Gabby was crying because you scared her. And you're scaring me."

She cups my cheek. "Oh, my sweet boy. You don't need to

worry so much. I'll be just fine. Now, I'll write it down that I need to talk to the doctor about this at my appointment on Thursday."

"Monday," I correct her, and she nods.

"That's right, Monday."

I'LL TRY TO get some time off on Monday so I can take Mom to the doctor. I don't trust that she'll remember to talk to him about this, and it's clearly getting much worse."

"I'm so sorry, Quinn." Sienna links her fingers through mine, and I immediately feel calmer. "Watching those we love age is hard. My dad had a heart attack two years ago, and I was a mess with worry."

"It's tough," I agree. "And it seems to be snowballing with her. A year ago, she was fit as a fiddle, and now her blood pressure is through the roof, her joints ache, and she can't remember who anyone is."

"There has to be an explanation," she says reasonably. "I hope the doctor has some answers for you."

"Me too. Now that we've lost most of the afternoon, *and* we made headway with finding that receipt today, let's play hooky. I'll take you out to dinner."

"We could get dinner to go and eat while we work," she suggests.

"No." I kiss the back of her hand. "No, I want to be with you this evening, just the two of us, without work or family obligations."

She takes a minute to answer, but finally says, "So, as fun as that sounds, I can't. I'm sorry, I have plans with Louise tonight."

I frown, disappointment hot and swift in my belly.

"Plans can be changed."

She looks over at me, then shakes her head.

"Sorry. I've had these plans with her for a couple of weeks. We're having dinner at my place, and drinking wine."

And I've just found a new level of respect for Sienna. She's not the kind of girl to drop everything in her life for a man.

I may not like the idea of not spending time with her tonight, but I respect her immensely.

"But I'll see you tomorrow," she says with a smile.

"Tomorrow it is."

Chapter Nine

~Sienna~

*Y*ou're late," I call out when I hear the front door open and close. My back is to Lou while I get the pizza ready for the oven.

"Girl, I got here as fast as I could."

I pause at the voice, then spin and run into strong, outstretched arms. Rich rocks me back and forth, then plants a kiss square on my cheek.

"Oh my God, Lou didn't say you were in town."

"It's a surprise," Lou says with a happy smile. She sets two bottles of wine on the island, then opens the oven to get a look at the pizza. "I hope you have more food than this."

"Of course I do." I pass the corkscrew and wine to Rich. "Will you do the honors?"

"Happily."

Rich and Louise have been best friends since they were kids. He came out to Lou first when they were fourteen, and he's been there for her through failed relationships, job changes, you name it.

They're as tight as it gets.

And because of that, Rich was at our house all the time while we were growing up.

"How's Boston?" I ask him and pull out the fixings for another pizza.

"I like it," he says with a nod. His dark hair is long enough to fall in his eyes as he opens the second bottle of wine. "My job is excellent."

"Have you met anyone interesting?"

He smiles slyly. "Honey, I always meet interesting people."

"Interesting enough to see them naked?" Lou asks with a wink.

"Not many of those," Rich replies with a sigh. "LouLou and I always have bad luck when it comes to men."

"You can say that again," Lou says, raising her glass in a toast.

"You just waste your time on the wrong people," I reply as I check the first pizza, then sip my glass of red. "Seriously, if he asks for your credit card number on the second date, it's time to move on."

"Easy for you to say, *Counselor*," Rich says.

"Just because I'm a lawyer doesn't mean it's easy to meet men. In fact, I date less than anyone else I know."

"Well, until recently." Louise smiles innocently as Rich's jaw drops and he covers his heart with a hand.

"You're holding out on me. Now, let's sit and you can tell me *everything*. Starting with, is he hot naked?"

I look at Lou, who just raises a brow and sips more wine.

"You don't know that I've seen him naked."

They look at each other and say in unison, "She's seen him naked."

"We are *not* talking about me," I remind them and pull the first pizza out of the oven, then slip the other one inside. I keep my eyes on the cheesy goodness as I run the cutter over it. "We're talking about you."

"Not anymore," Louise says. "Our love lives are boring. Catch Rich up. Unless you want me to."

"You do it," Rich says. "She leaves out the good parts."

I roll my eyes and pull down plates.

"So this hot lawyer showed up at our grandfather's will reading." Lou continues with the story, up to last night when we went to the show.

She doesn't know anything past that because I haven't had a chance to see her.

"So, let me get this straight. He's a hot, rich attorney, and his brother's girlfriend is London Watson."

"Fiancée now," I reply with a smile. "They got engaged today."

"Of course," Rich says with a nod. "What happened after the show?"

I smile slowly, and both Lou and Rich start to clap and woot in excitement.

"You banged the hot lawyer!" Louise exclaims.

"His name is *Quinn*," I reply and take another sip of wine, then fill my glass again. "And yes, I totally banged him. A few times."

"Holy shit," she says with a sigh. "That's awesome."

"There's more."

I tell them about breaking my heel, and needing new shoes. The Louboutins. Dinner. His condo with my painting hanging in it.

"Fucking hell, *I'm* in love with him," Rich says, fanning his face as he chews his pizza. "Seriously, if you don't claim him, I'll take him."

"I don't think he bats for your team," I reply with a laugh. "And no one said anything about love. But he is sexy, and he's really . . . *swoony.*"

"I like that word," Lou says with a happy sigh. "And if he ever starts to be not swoony, I'm gonna kick him in the balls."

"That seems extreme."

She shrugs a shoulder. "I'm serious. You're the nicest person in the universe."

"That's totally not true," I reply.

We've moved into the living room, with pizza and wine, and for the next hour, we giggle and drink, just like the old days.

It's not long before I realize that I can see two of each of them.

"This wine is potent."

"Damn right," Lou says. "I have more in the car. Hold, please."

She jumps up and runs out the door before I can say anything. We hear a door slam, and then she's back, carrying two more bottles.

"Jesus, I'm already drunk, Lou."

"Good, we're well on our way to shitfaced."

"Is that the goal?" I ask.

"Of course it is," Rich says and opens another bottle. "Now, we've talked about jobs and boys, let's talk about boys."

We snort laugh, and I watch as he fills my glass again.

"I don't have anything else to say. But I kind of miss him. Maybe I should text him."

"Don't be that girl," Lou says while shaking her head. "Don't say I love you in a text."

"That's definitely *not* what I was going to say," I reply. "I know, I'll take a selfie and send him that."

I open his last text, and then the little camera icon. I hit the circle, but instead of taking a photo, it starts ringing.

"Shit, I'm facetiming him."

"Even better," Rich says as Quinn picks up.

"Hey," he says with a smile.

"Sorry, this isn't what I meant to do."

I hang up on him, and try again for a photo, but it just calls him again.

"Are you okay?" he asks when he picks up.

"Oh, I'm fine, I just think my phone is against me. I'm trying to send you a photo. Not a naked one."

"How many glasses of wine have you had?"

"I dunno." I look down at him and grin. "You're so handsome. What are you wearing?"

A smile slides over his lips, and I wish he was here. I want to kiss him.

"I'm just in my usual."

"I want to see his usual," Rich whispers to Lou, and I shush him.

Quinn pans down so I can see his cargo shorts and his T-shirt.

Yum.

"We should make pancakes," Lou says, getting my attention, and my focus immediately shifts.

"Pancakes! Sorry, Quinn, I gotta go."

I hang up on him, and toss my phone away, immediately craving soft, fluffy pancakes.

"I should stop drinking," I announce and stand, holding my hands out to get my balance. "And eat pancakes because they'll soak up the drunk."

"Do you have the stuff?" Lou asks, joining me in the kitchen.

"Of course. Hold on." I open the pantry and pull out my electric skillet and a box of pancake mix, and get to work. "This is gonna be awesome."

"I'm still going to drink," Rich says, pouring himself more wine. "Because I'm not a quitter."

Louise and I blow raspberries as we giggle at Rich's joke.

"Good one."

It takes about an hour to make the pancakes because we keep messing up. They're too burnt, they're not cooked enough. They fall apart because I forgot eggs.

It's a mess and a riot, all at the same time.

Finally, I'm not as fuzzy as I was, and I'm able to pull off six perfect pancakes.

"So good," I mumble around a mouthful of maple goodness.

"The best," Lou agrees.

My doorbell rings, and I frown as I hurry across the living room and swing the door open.

"Quinn."

He's grinning, standing there in his cargo shorts and T-shirt, and I instinctively lick my lips.

Because he's damn hot.

"I thought I wasn't going to see you until tomorrow."

He checks his watch. "It's 12:22. It *is* tomorrow."

I take his hand and pull him into my house. "So it is. Good thinking. I'm warning you, I've been drinking, and although I've sobered up a little thanks to the pancakes, we're silly."

"I can live with silly." He tucks a piece of my hair behind my ear, and all my lady parts sit up and take notice.

Every. Single. Lady. Part.

"Is this him?" Rich asks, and Quinn's grip on my hand tightens. "Because *hello, Counselor.*"

I giggle and then shrug helplessly. "Rich might flirt with you. I apologize in advance."

His whole body seems to relax with my words, and then he just shakes his head and chuckles, holding his hand out to Rich.

"I'm Quinn."

"And I'm single," Rich says with a wink, making Lou and me laugh, and Quinn's cheeks go red. "But I can see that you're taken. Pity. I'm Rich, LouLou's fabulous best friend."

"Nice to meet you." Quinn glances down at me. "Did you mention pancakes?"

"Yeah, do you want some?"

"Definitely."

WHAT DOES A girl do when she has a hangover the size of Manhattan and can't sleep?

Well, this girl paints.

It's superearly in the morning, before sunrise. Quinn was out cold next to me, his arm slung over my waist. Lou and Rich were asleep on the pullout couch. Everyone was full of pancakes, wine, and happiness.

My insomnia isn't from stress, or worry. I'm not uncomfortable with Quinn being in my bed. If anything, I'm more comfortable than I thought I would be.

I just couldn't sleep.

So I slipped into my studio about an hour ago, shut the door, and turned on the lights, and I've been powering through this headache with my watercolors.

I should work on the park painting, but I'm not in the mood for the harshness of the oils. That's for when I'm upset.

So instead I pulled out a new canvas, and I'm working from memory. I love painting ocean scenes. They're harder than you'd think, and they're different every time.

Today I'm painting Cannon Beach on the Oregon coast. We went there when I was a teenager for a family vacation, and I fell in love with it. I'm convinced that I'll retire there one day.

I have the sand and Haystack Rock outlined, and I've just reached for the blues for the water when there's a soft knock, and then Quinn comes inside.

"Why are you awake?" he whispers, crossing to me and planting his lips on my forehead.

"Good question," I reply. "I don't know, I just couldn't fall asleep. So I thought this might make me sleepy."

"Do you mind if I watch?"

His eyes are heavy with slumber, his hair a mess from my pillows.

"I'll come back to bed with you," I offer.

"It's up to you. If you want to paint, I'll watch. Or leave you. I just woke up and you were gone, so I wanted to check on you. Make sure you weren't throwing up or anything."

"Ew." I wrinkle my nose. "I don't think that's something I want you to witness. Ever. I do have a hell of a headache, but otherwise, I'm okay."

"Not tired?"

"I'm tired, but restless. That's the best way to describe it. I was in the mood for watercolors."

I explain the differences for me in the mediums, and when I glance over at him, his lips are turned up in a soft smile. His brown eyes are happy.

And aside from the boxers he threw on, he's naked. And I'm suddenly no longer interested in painting.

"We should go down to bed," I say, putting my supplies away, and reaching for his hand. "Honest, now that you're awake, I can think of a better way to occupy our time at this hour."

"I won't say no to that."

SOMEONE IS JACKHAMMERING my brain.

"You have to wake up, sweetness."

"Why are you screaming at me?" I demand from under my pillow.

Quinn chuckles, and I can smell coffee, so I peek out from under the pillow to find not just the room bathed in sunlight, but a smiling Quinn Cavanaugh as well.

"Good morning," he says.

"How is my hangover worse than it was when you found me in my studio? Isn't sex supposed to cure it?"

"Sex cures a lot of things," he says as he pulls the pillow completely off me, making me frown. "But you need to hydrate to get rid of the headache."

"Do you have coffee?" There's no masking the hope in my voice.

"I brought you some," he confirms, and I sit up, reaching out for it, but he holds it just beyond my fingertips. "In exchange for a kiss."

"I can't do cute flirting in the morning when I'm hungover and haven't had coffee, ace."

"Did you just call me *ace*?"

"It suits you," I reply, taking the coffee from him and a long sip. The caffeine immediately hits my veins and I sigh in happiness. "That's better already."

"You slept a long time."

"What time is it?"

"Ten."

I feel my eyes go wide. "*Ten?*"

"You obviously needed the sleep."

I shake my head and climb out of the bed, trying to keep my coffee in my hand and cover my nakedness, but it's no use. I need more hands.

So I let the covers fall and take a sip of coffee.

There's no prying this out of my hands.

"Jesus," Quinn whispers and leans in to tug a nipple between his lips. I feel the zing through my belly to my clit, and I have to steady myself on his shoulder.

"No time for this," I mutter, but I don't move away when he tugs it in his mouth for a second time.

"You shouldn't walk around naked if you don't want my hands on you," he says.

"Those are lips, not hands."

"Semantics," he replies, but pulls away and doesn't try to entice me back into the bed as I pull on some clothes and pull my hair into its usual knot.

"Are Rich and Lou still here?"

"Yeah, Lou was making more pancakes."

I cringe. "God, I don't know if I can ever have pancakes again. And that's sad because I love pancakes."

I cross to Quinn, who's still sitting at the edge of my bed, and pull him in for a big hug. "Thanks for staying with me last night, and for the coffee."

"You're welcome."

"I guess we should go upstairs."

"Lead the way," he replies.

Rich and Louise are indeed in my kitchen, eating pancakes and showing each other photos on their phones.

"Good morning, sunshine," Rich says with a smile.

"Why do you look like that?" Louise demands.

"Like what? I'm hungover, how am I supposed to look?" I inspect both of them and then scowl. "Why aren't you guys hungover?"

"We never get hungover," Rich says with a shrug.

"You should drink a bunch of water," Lou says with a sage nod. "That'll help a lot."

All I can do is flip her the bird, feeling not a little betrayed that neither of them feel like shit, especially when the sexy man I'm interested in is standing right beside me.

Jerks.

"I made pancakes," Louise says. "That might help you feel better."

"No." I shake my head and take a sip of my coffee, which is cooling off. "I can't do pancakes."

"How about an omelet?" Quinn asks, catching my attention.

"Oh, that actually sounds good."

"You got it. Sit down, I'll get you a bottle of water, and make you the omelet."

"I'd like an omelet," Rich says.

"Then I guess you'll have to make yourself one," Quinn says and winks at me. "I'm too busy taking care of my girl."

"Okay, there he goes, being swoony again," Lou says with a wide smile.

"Swoony?" Quinn asks.

"Ignore them," I say before Louise can respond. "They're both dumb. And they definitely don't deserve your omelet."

"We have to run anyway," Lou says as she and Rich stand and gather their things. "But I'll call you later."

"It was good to see you, sugar pie." Rich hugs me tightly, then nods at Quinn. "Be nice to her, or Lou will kick you in the balls."

"Um, okay," Quinn replies.

"It's a thing," Louise agrees with a smile as she waves and leaves with Rich.

"Oh, come on, you're an attorney. Surely you've had your family jewels threatened before." Quinn sets my omelet before me and then leans on the countertop, thinking it over.

"Once or twice, but typically not while they had a smug smile on their face."

I can't help but laugh, then sigh from the dull ache behind my eyes.

"Seriously, sweetheart, drink some water. It'll help."

He opens the bottle for me, and I take a long drink. "Thank you, for all this."

"You're welcome. We should get ready to head out. We have to go to work today."

I glare at him. "Not today, Satan."

"Yes, today." He laughs and makes himself an omelet. "We still have three-quarters of the boxes in the attic to go through, and time's slipping away on the deadline."

I sigh and brace my face in my hand. "You're right. I never thought I'd be so sick of paper in my life. It's tedious."

"But it's paying off," he reminds me and leans over to kiss my temple. "You're finding your proof, and I get to spend time with you. It's a win-win."

"But what about *you* winning?" I ask, frowning at him.

"As long as we find the truth, we both win. That's what matters here."

"You *are* swoony."

"I have my moments," he agrees with a smug smile. "And after work today, I want to take you somewhere fun."

"Am I going to need a safety harness? A helmet?"

"God, I hope so."

Chapter Ten

~Sienna~

I love the zoo," I say with a wide smile as Quinn pulls into the Bronx Zoo parking. "This will be great. I need to take a long walk."

"We're not here to see the animals," he says as he takes my hand and pulls me out of his Porsche, locks the car, and leads me toward the entrance.

"Then why in the world are we at the zoo?"

"Zip lining."

I stop in my tracks, pulling him to a stop with me.

"No."

I shake my head adamantly, but Quinn laughs, kisses my hand, and nudges me to keep walking.

"It'll be fun. Fresh air is exactly what we need after spending all this time around dusty papers."

"I'm afraid of heights," I admit and bite my lip, already

dreading this. "Seriously, you can zip-line, and I'll cheer you on and then we can go see the tigers."

"*You* zip-line and then I'll take you to see the tigers."

We approach the gate and he pays for two passes, for both the zoo and the zip lining, and I follow him inside.

"Quinn—"

He pulls me into his arms now, holding me in a tight hug, his hands rubbing up and down my back. "Sienna, you're the fiercest woman I know. You can do this."

"I know, I just don't want to." I take a deep breath, snuggling against him, and then let it out slowly. I'm pouting, and I know it. I've never faced so many fears in my life like I have in just the short time I've known Quinn.

It's actually kind of badass. He's right, I *can* do it. And if it makes him happy in the process, what's the harm?

He chuckles and kisses my forehead. "Let's go check it out. If it still freaks you out, we'll go see the tigers."

"I don't understand what's so exciting about being three hundred feet in the air." My voice isn't pouty now, but more curious.

"I wish this were that high up," he says with a sigh. "Unfortunately, we're restricted by the city, and this one is only about forty feet off the ground."

"Only. I could still fall to my death."

"You won't," he says with the confidence that only Quinn has. "Not to mention, this is a side-by-side line, so we can go at the same time."

"Is that supposed to be encouraging?"

He grins and winks. "Yep."

Just then, two people sail over us, laughing and whooping.

"See? They're having fun."

"They looked sixteen."

"This is a sport for all ages," he assures me.

"I warned you that I'm not a thrill seeker."

He frowns, and I feel a bit guilty. He's trying to include me in things that he likes to do for fun, and given that the man is a workaholic who doesn't get out of the office much, he's not only taking time off, he's including me.

And that says a lot.

"But I'm going to try it."

His face transforms back into a smile.

"Thank you."

I take a deep breath when we approach the guys in their gear, and the next thirty minutes is full of fittings and instructions.

"Here's your helmet," Quinn says, passing it to me. I try to put it on my head, but my bun is in the way. "You'll have to take your hair down."

I wrinkle my nose, but do as he says and tuck my hair tie in my pocket. The helmet slips on easily, fastening under my chin.

"You look cute in this outfit."

"Oh good, because that's what I was going for."

Quinn laughs and takes out his phone, snapping a selfie of the two of us, and then we're on a platform, looking down forty feet to the ground.

"It's really high."

"I've zip-lined five hundred feet in the air before," Quinn says, shaking his head. "This is an easy one."

"Goodie," I mutter under my breath. *I'm going to die. This is how it happens.*

"Hey." I glance over at Quinn, who's smiling at me, and holding his hand out for mine, which I take. "I'm going to be right next to you the whole way. Don't close your eyes because you'll miss it."

"Yes, sir."

And the next thing I know, we're sailing through the air, held up with only some cables and sheer will, and it's . . . *exhilarating.*

Fun, even.

"Holy shit!" I call out. Our arms are stretched out as we sail, both of us laughing and looking at the zoo, the trees around us. It's magnificent.

And something I never would have done without Quinn.

We go on three more runs, and then the gear is taken off me, the helmet unfastened, and I immediately twist my hair back up.

"You should wear it down," Quinn says casually. "I like your hair."

"It gets in my way," I say and take his offered hand. "Are we going to see the tigers now?"

"A promise is a promise."

"That's right. Also, I want a churro and a Coke."

"Now you're asking a lot."

"Hey, I conquered my fear of heights for you."

"A churro and a Coke it is."

"Is it Wednesday already?" I check the calendar on my desk when Uncle Patrick walks into my tiny office and sits in the chair next to my desk. I came to the office today for research and for a change of scenery. "Time is flying by."

"Wednesday at noon," he confirms with a wink. He looks so much like Grandpa, the way I remember him from when I was small. "But instead of going out today, I brought lunch to you."

He sets a brown bag on my desk, and we dig into sandwiches and pickles.

"Thank you for this."

"I know you've been busier than normal," he says and takes a sip of his water. "How is the case going, by the way?"

"Not bad, actually." I take a bite of my sandwich, surprised at just how hungry I was. "But it's slow going."

"Do you need anything?"

"I don't think so." I wipe my mouth and my phone rings. "Do you mind if I take this?"

"Of course not."

"This is Sienna."

"Hi, Sienna, it's London. I'm sure you're at work, and I don't mean to interrupt."

"No worries, London. What's up?"

"Well, the guys are working late today, and I thought you

and I could meet up for a drink when you're finished for the day? There's a great place near Finn's office that has the *best* martinis in town."

"That actually sounds like a lot of fun. I'd love to. Can I text you when I'm leaving here?"

"That's perfect. I'm excited to see you."

"Same here, see you soon."

I hang up and turn to Uncle Patrick, who's watching me curiously. I'm sure he could hear most of my conversation. My office is so small we're practically bumping elbows.

"I thought you were working on the park case in the evenings," he says.

"I am, but Quinn has to work late with his brother, so I'm going to meet with London, Quinn's brother's fiancée, for drinks until Quinn's free."

"In the city, where the files aren't."

I sit back and wipe my mouth again, watching him steadily. "Yes."

"Sienna, I don't know that it's appropriate for you to be working so closely with the opposing counsel of a case. I would hate to see you get thrown off the case because you're acting . . . inappropriately."

I chew a bite of my pickle, surprised at both my uncle's opinion, and my immediate need to defend myself.

"Well, although Quinn and I are working for different sides of the same case, we are working toward the same goal: to find the truth. Not to mention, the judge okayed us working together.

This case is over a hundred years old, Uncle Patrick. There's no way that I could do all this work alone."

"I'm simply voicing my concerns."

"And you have." I toss my wrapper in the trashcan, irritated that he's questioning my motives and my work ethic. He knows that my family and this case are important to me. "I wouldn't do anything to mess this up. It's important to me, our family, *and* the city. So believe me when I say that I'm motivated to win this case, and who I choose to spend my free time with won't affect that."

"Good." His face is sober as he stands. "I know you have a heavy workload, and I won't keep you longer. I'd appreciate it if you'd keep me posted on this."

"You know I can't do that." I frown up at him, and finally stand. "I can't tell you much."

He winks. "We can talk privately."

"Whether we're in my office or in your house, the answer is the same."

He nods, then turns and walks out of my office, and I'm left wondering what the hell just happened. Uncle Patrick knows that I can't talk about the case, and he's never questioned my judgment before.

Is it grief talking? Concern? I don't know, but I don't like it.

"Over here!"

London's by the windows, waving in my direction. Her long, dark hair is down and curly, and her smile is wide and friendly.

Yes, I think London and I are going to be friends.

"Hey, sorry it took so long for me to get here. Traffic was a bitch." I set my handbag in the chair next to me and sit down.

"You're fine, and I took the liberty of ordering you a lemon drop."

"Bless you." I sigh and take a sip of my cocktail. London reaches up to tuck her hair behind her ear, and I immediately make grabby hands. "First things first. I need to see this ring."

"He's a crazy man," she says with a laugh, holding her hand out for me to ogle the sparkly diamond on her finger.

"It looks better on you than it did in the box."

"Did he show you?"

I nod and sip my drink. "He was nervous, and I told him that with a ring like that, he had nothing to worry about."

"He could have given me a Cracker Jack ring and I still would have said yes," she replies, looking dreamily at her hand. "But he did good."

"How did he propose? He said you guys were going to Martha's Vineyard, but that's all I know."

"Well, we fell in love there," she begins. "We own houses next door to each other, and we both spent a lot of time there last year."

"The ol' next-door neighbor trick," I say with a nod, making her laugh.

"Exactly. We hadn't been back there in a long while because we've both been so busy with work, so when he suggested that we fly over for the weekend after opening night, I jumped at it. I miss the beach so much."

"The beach is the best. I haven't been in years."

"Oh, you guys should go stay in one of our places. You're welcome anytime."

"Thank you. Now, get to the good stuff."

"Right." She laughs and shifts in her chair. "So, a storm was rolling in, and I'm horribly afraid of storms. Like, my anxiety kicks up, and I'm a wreck. It's been that way since I was a kid.

"Finn knows this, of course, and he's great at calming me down. Usually, he just distracts me with his naked antics, and it works marvelously."

"As it should."

"I do like you," she says with a laugh. "Anyway, we'd been at the house for a couple of hours, and it was late because the show went late, and it was chaotic. So, we're lying in bed, and I can see the lightning, and I'm starting to get keyed up. Finn starts the whole naked antics thing—"

"Bless him."

"And then he stops, and he's, like, *I was going to do this tomorrow on the beach, but I just can't wait.* And he asked me to marry him."

"Well, that's one way to distract you from the storm."

"Right? I don't think I'll ever see a storm and not think of that moment. It was special."

"What are you going to tell other people when they ask you how he proposed?"

"I can't exactly say he asked me during naked antics," she says, biting her lip. "I guess I'll just say he asked me at the beach. It's true."

"Perfect." I hold my glass up to clink against hers. "Congratulations."

"Thank you. Now, let's talk about you and Quinn."

"There have been some naked antics," I concede, making her snort.

"It looked like more than that at the opening," she says. "I saw the way he looked at you."

"And how is that?"

"Like you hung the moon and every star in the sky."

"I like him," I reply and shrug one shoulder. "We're spending a lot of time together because of this case. I don't know what will happen when it's over."

"Why?"

"He'll go back to working eighty hours a week, of course."

"Maybe he won't. Finn has learned how to balance both."

"I don't know if Quinn wants that," I reply thoughtfully. "He loves the thrill of his job."

"And he can still have that," she points out. "Don't write him off so easily. Sometimes a person is willing to do more than they thought possible with the right motivation."

"You never know," I agree. "I'm not writing him off. I guess I'm just taking it one day at a time."

"Nothing wrong with that either."

"We found you."

Finn and Quinn approach the table. Finn kisses London passionately, and I turn to Quinn with a smile, but I'm swept up as well, in a hot kiss that makes my toes curl in my fancy Louboutins.

"Well, hello there," I say when he pulls away.

"Hi. I brought you these." He passes me roses with white petals that turn to pink at the tips. "It's my apology for being late."

"You're forgiven." I bury my nose in them and breathe deeply. "They'll look great in my studio."

"Quinn told us that you're an artist, Sienna," Finn says after he and Quinn order beers. "I saw the painting hanging in his condo."

"Did you paint that?" London asks with wide eyes.

"I did," I confirm.

"It's beautiful. Do you ever do custom work?"

"I haven't before, but I don't see why I couldn't."

"Oh, I'd love a painting of the beach house to hang in our Manhattan home," she says, clapping her hands in excitement. "We don't go there often enough. Could you work from photos?"

"Why don't we go there?" Quinn asks, surprising me.

"Because we're in the middle of a case?"

He shrugs one shoulder and takes a sip of his beer. "When the case is done, we could take a weekend and go."

"You really should," Finn says. "It's beautiful there, and then you can see the house in person. You can even paint there, if you want."

"I have a great sunroom," London says, opening the photos on her phone and turns the screen to me, showing me an enclosed porch with a view of the water.

"That would be a great place to paint."

"It's settled then," Quinn says and links his fingers with mine under the table. "We'll get the case finished up, and then we'll slip away for a few days."

"Okay." I nod, thinking it over. "I had to reschedule my vacation time for this case, I'm sure I can talk my boss into extending my sabbatical with vacation. I'll take a week off work, and when we get back, I'll finish your painting."

"Do you want me to pay you in advance?" London asks, but I shake my head.

"Consider it an engagement present."

London's eyes fill with tears, and Quinn lifts my hand to his lips.

"I like her," London says, dabbing at her eyes. "She's a keeper."

"I like her too," Quinn replies, watching me with those brown eyes. "Thank you."

"You might hate it," I reply, trying to lighten the mood again.

"I'll love it," she says with a sniff, then smiles brightly. "Now, let's toast to new beginnings and new friends."

"I'll drink to that."

The waitress returns to ask us if we'd like to order food.

"Should we order something?" Finn asks, but Quinn is already shaking his head no.

"We have to go to work," he says and winks at me.

"Thanks for the drinks, and congratulations again," I say as London comes around the table to give me a hug. "Let's do this again."

"I'm holding you to that," she says. "And when you're ready to head to the beach, Quinn and Finn will arrange it."

"Thank you."

We walk out of the bar and down the block to Quinn's office building, then down to the parking garage.

"Are you sure you want to drive into the Bronx at this time?" I ask him, checking my watch. "That'll put you home really late."

"I hate to lose another day of work, but what I really want to do is take you home, get you naked, and make you scream."

My whole body tenses, and my panties flood. Jesus, he can take me from pleasantly content to raging horniness in the span of seven words.

"Um, well, that sounds like fun too."

He laughs, kisses my hand again, and drives smoothly through Manhattan traffic to his building.

"Of course, you're going to have to feed me."

"Sex and food, in that order."

Chapter Eleven

~Quinn~

*N*ow that we've wrapped that up," Bruce House says and shifts his papers on my conference table, "let's talk about the property in the Bronx. How is the case going?"

This is how I spend every Friday morning, with Bruce in the conference room, going over the several cases that I'm working on for him at any given time.

The man owns half of Manhattan.

"It's progressing," I reply. "Ms. Hendricks, the family's attorney, has found two receipts of payments on the original loan, showing payment of fifty percent."

His eyebrows climb and he sits back in his chair, thinking.

"Interesting. So it's conceivable that the loan was paid in full after all."

It's probable. "Agreed."

"The city attorney's name is Hendricks?"

I narrow my eyes, watching as he rubs his fingertips over his lips.

"You know it is, you met her."

"I honestly didn't remember her name at the time, but it occurs to me that the last name of the person who sent me the letter was Hendricks."

Every hair on my body stands on end.

"And you're realizing that *now*?"

He shrugs a shoulder. "It didn't seem important at the time."

"It's called *Hendricks Park*, the attorney's name is Hendricks, and you didn't connect the dots that the person who gave you this letter is also Hendricks?"

He stares at me for a moment, not answering, and I want to throw something.

"Bruce."

"Okay, I didn't say anything," he says and holds his hands up in surrender. "I am now."

"I can't represent you if you withhold information."

He holds my gaze steadily. "You have the information."

"What was the first name?"

"Patrick," he says, and my blood is officially boiling. "Is he a relative of hers?"

"I don't know," I reply, lying easily. I'm not giving Bruce personal information on Sienna. "I'll keep you posted on any changes in the case."

"I know."

He gathers his things, and just as he is every Friday, he's out the door by ten.

And I immediately walk into Finn's office, pleased to see that Carter's already here.

"I need to talk to you two."

I shut the door and lock it, earning intrigued looks from both of them.

"What's up?" Carter asks and takes a sip of coffee.

"Bruce House is a pain in my ass, and I don't know why I work for him."

"Because he brings millions of dollars into our practice every year," Finn replies reasonably. "What did he do now?"

"He withheld important information on the Bronx case. He just told me it was *Patrick Hendricks* who gave him the original letter of sale."

"Who's Patrick Hendricks?" Finn asks.

"Sienna's uncle."

They exchange looks of surprise, and I want to punch something all over again.

"Why didn't he tell you that weeks ago?"

"Why does Bruce do *anything* he does?" I respond and pace to the windows. "But now I know that Sienna's fucking *uncle* is trying to sabotage ownership of the park. She's going to be so hurt. She's close to him."

"Quinn, you can't tell her." I turn at Carter's comment and shove my hands in my pockets, dread settling heavy in my belly. "Attorney-client privilege. You can't tell her."

"I'm fucked," I reply and sit in the leather chair next to Carter, then hang my head in my hands. "How am I supposed to look her in the eye and keep this from her?"

"What's really going on between you two?" Carter asks. "Surely it's not more than sex."

"I'm head over heels in love with her," I reply immediately, surprising all three of us. I stare at each of them, my mouth opening and closing, and then I swallow hard and rub my hand down my face. "Yeah, I am."

"Jesus," Finn whispers. "I knew it. I've never seen you look at anyone like that."

"So, I know that her uncle is fucking her over, and I can't tell her."

"No," Carter replies. "You can't."

"What do you have so far?" Finn asks, and I repeat what I told Bruce, that we've found 50 percent of the money.

"But we've only gone through a quarter of the boxes, and we have two weeks left."

"We have to step up the pace with that," Finn says. "We have law clerks that can go through the paperwork."

"You're right," I reply, nodding. "We *have* to find the proof that the money was paid back. I'll just have all the boxes brought here, and we can have the clerks do it."

"Good luck with that," Carter says with a smirk. "Like Sienna's just going to hand all of her family's paperwork from the past hundred years to the opposing counsel."

"I'll talk her into it," I reply. "She'll see reason."

"Like I said, good luck with that."

I immediately hurry back to my own office, lock the door, and call Sienna.

"This is Sienna."

"It's me. Listen, I was looking at the calendar, and the stack of boxes we still have to go through, and it occurs to me that time is working against us."

"I already know this," she says with a sigh.

"Well, I was thinking, why don't I have all the remaining boxes moved to my offices, and I can assign several law clerks to start helping."

She's quiet for a minute, and just when I think I've dropped the call, my phone starts to ring with a FaceTime.

"Are you nuts?" she asks when I pick up.

"I don't think so."

"Quinn, I'm not going to just hand over all my family's information to your office. The fact that I've invited *you* to help me was a huge step for me."

Okay, so Carter was right.

"Sienna, there's no way we'll finish on time at this pace. We need more man power. Even with you working full-time, and me helping part-time, it's not enough."

She blows out a breath and closes her eyes, and I wish I was there to hold her hand, or wrap her in my arms. But she doesn't need that. She needs to figure this out on her own.

Watching the emotions play over her beautiful face is fascinating. Finally, she sighs again and shakes her head, as if she doesn't believe what she's about to say. "Quinn, there are going to be rules."

"Understood and agreed. I'll arrange to have everything moved over on Monday morning."

"Okay. I'll see you later."

And then she's gone, and I set the plan into motion, hire the moving company, and assign the duties, using only senior clerks.

For all our sakes, I don't want anyone to fuck this up.

"Jesus, my eyes are blurry," Sienna says the next afternoon. She pushes her fingers against her eyes and sighs. We've been sitting at this table since the sun came up this morning, poring through boxes.

Still nothing.

I stand, stretch my legs, and walk to her, kneading her shoulders and neck.

"Oh, that's good." She sighs, leaning into my touch. "I know we should stay longer, but my brain is mush."

"It'll still be here tomorrow," I reply, leaning in to kiss the top of her head. "And we'll have plenty of help at the office starting on Monday."

"Are you sure it's a good idea?" she asks and leans back to look up at me. "It makes me nervous."

"What, you don't trust me?"

"You? Yes, without hesitation. But I don't know your clerks."

I fucking hate having this secret between us. Something tells me that once trust is broken with Sienna, repairing it is almost impossible.

But I don't have a choice.

"We'll lay the ground rules. Dave has given you the slack to work this case exclusively until it's done, so you'll be there every day. We're going to make it work."

"Okay," she says with a sigh. "We do need the help, that's for sure."

She stands and turns to hug me, tipping her face up for a kiss. Her lips are soft and smooth, and confident under mine.

She intoxicates me.

"I think it's my turn to take you somewhere special," she says with a smile.

"Do I need a safety harness? A helmet?" I turn her words back at her and she giggles, making my stomach—and my cock—clench.

"Not this time," she replies as she gathers her things and leads me out of the house, locking up, and joining me at my car. She moves to the passenger side, but I stop her.

"Why don't you drive?"

She stops and turns those big blue eyes to mine. "Me?"

"You." I grin and open the driver's-side door for her. "You know where we're going."

She looks longingly at the car, then smiles widely and hurries over to slide in behind the wheel.

"You don't have to tell me twice," she says as I sit in the passenger side and buckle my seat belt. "I won't speed too badly."

"I'm not worried," I reply with a laugh.

"Have you ever been pulled over?"

I look at her, then start to laugh from deep in my gut.

"More times than I can count." I grin as she gets the seat situated just so, adjusts the mirrors, then pushes the start button and eases onto the road.

Then she guns it, and we're off, speeding through the residential streets of the Bronx.

"You *do* love to go fast," I say, watching her bite her lip in excitement.

"This car is just . . . *so good*."

"You can drive it whenever we're together, if you want."

She giggles, glances over at me, then giggles again. The next thing I know, we're parked at her house.

"We're here," she announces, taking her belt off and climbing out of the car.

"We drove less than a mile," I say in surprise.

"Yep. This is where I wanted to go."

Before she can walk into the house, I catch her wrist and pull her against me, thrilled at the way her body molds against mine, as if she was made just for me.

"You're incredible. You know that, right?"

"I'm pretty okay," she agrees with a grin, gazing up at me with happy eyes. "Let's go inside."

I follow her into the house. She drops her bag and keys in their usual places. The rest of her house is in order. It's not perfect, the way it would be if she were a crazy neat freak, but most everything has a place.

"Do you need to pick something up?" I ask, but she shakes her head, leading me down to her bedroom. "Or did you just want to get naked?"

"Neither," she says with a laugh. "I want to take you to my studio. I need to change my clothes. Do you care if those that you're wearing get messy?"

I glance down at my usual weekend attire of cargo shorts and a T-shirt and shake my head. "No, I have a million of these."

"Excellent." She slips into her closet, and less than a minute later, she returns in a tiny pair of cutoffs and a white tank, both with paint spatter on them. "This is my painting outfit."

"Jesus, Sienna, I'll have you naked before we get to the top of the stairs."

She grins and shakes her head, and I can't stop staring at her.

Her feet are bare, her strawberry-blond hair is twisted up in its usual casual knot, and she's wearing her glasses, which immediately makes my dick hard.

Add in the paint outfit, and I'm ready to fucking explode.

"I want to do this with you," she says as she takes my hand and leads me up the stairs and to the studio. Natural light is flooding the space. She has tarps thrown on the floor, protecting it from paint.

And she has two brand-new canvases set up on easels in the middle of the room.

"Did you plan this?"

"Maybe," she says with a grin. She has two clean paint palettes set on a table and begins to load them with the same colors of paints. "We're going to work on the same painting today. I'd like to teach you, if you want to learn."

"I'm all yours," I reply. Jesus, she's gorgeous, confident in every move she makes. Her motions are swift and precise, and before long, she has both palettes ready.

"Okay, here are your paints. I have brushes and water already set up at the easels."

"You're quite prepared."

"I haven't had a chance to paint much lately, and I was hoping we'd wrap it up early today. Besides, you've taken me several times to share what you enjoy, and I realized that I haven't done the same for you."

"I enjoy just being with you." She stops and turns to me, a happy smile spreading over her lips.

"That's a sweet thing to say."

"It's true. If I can race, or zip-line, or paint, or just breathe with you, well, it's all bonus."

"You're charming," she says as she preps both of our canvases.

"No, I'm not. I don't spew bullshit. I don't say what I don't mean."

"That's not what I was saying," she replies calmly. "I just meant that you're kind, and sweet, and it's quite attractive."

I blink, staring down at her as she pushes her glasses up the bridge of her little nose.

"Seems you don't spew bullshit either."

"Nope. Ain't nobody got time for that."

My lips twitch as I mimic what she's doing with her paints on my own canvas. "Am I doing this right?"

"Perfectly."

She starts to explain why she's preparing the canvases in a certain way. Why she chose these particular paints, and what she has in mind for us to paint today.

"I'd like to paint a skyline," she says. "It sounds simple, but it's not."

"None of this is simple," I reply, already frustrated and feeling like I have two left thumbs. "Who says it's simple?"

"I've found that many people brush the arts off as being *easy*. 'Oh, you write? I have an idea for a book.' 'Oh, you paint? I thought about doing that.'"

"Maybe they just wish they had the same talent that you do."

She tilts her head, thinking it over. "Maybe. It's a shame that we mock what we wish we had, isn't it?"

"Human beings do a lot of things that are shameful."

Like lie to their girlfriend about her asshole of an uncle.

She wipes her hand on her thigh, just under the hem of her shorts, and leaves a white streak of paint on her skin.

I don't know if I've ever seen anything so sexy in all my life.

For the next thirty minutes, we paint in silence. Sienna with sure strokes, confident lines, and me just trying to do my best.

The third time she wipes paint on her skin, this time on her chest just under her collarbone, I can't stand it anymore.

I set my paints on the table next to my easel, turn to her, and run my brush from the ball of her shoulder to her elbow.

Rather than gasp and freak out, which is exactly what I'm expecting her to do, she cocks an eyebrow, and stares down at the paint, then up at me through those black-rimmed glasses.

"Did you just paint me?"

"You're much more intriguing than the canvas."

She bites her lip, turns to me, and paints a blue line down my jaw. "You're right."

I load my brush with red paint this time, and make a heart in her cleavage, and then it's on.

I've forgotten all about the canvas, and I'm focused completely on the amazing woman before me.

"Take your shirt off," I command, not leaving room for argument. She complies immediately, and I swirl the paint over her puckered nipples, making them stand tall. Her skin breaks out into goose bumps.

"That's cold," she whispers. "But it feels . . . *good*."

Her body is magical. She smells like vanilla and spice, and her skin is smooth and soft. She's curvy in all the right places, and firm in others. She's every fantasy I've ever had, and exactly what I didn't know I was looking for.

"I'll never get tired of exploring you," I murmur, letting my brush trail over her shoulder to her back as I walk around her. "You're stunning, Sienna."

She sighs as I unfasten her shorts and let them pool around

her feet and continue to paint her skin, drawing patterns on her ass cheeks, her back, down her legs.

I'm careful to leave her core clean.

"Do I get to paint you now?" she asks breathlessly, making me grin.

"You can do whatever you want, sweetheart."

Rather than turn to me and start brushing paint over me, she drops her brush to the floor, turns to me, and launches herself into my arms.

I don't care that she's getting paint all over me, I only care that she's pressed against me, and I'm going to be inside her in about fourteen seconds.

Her fingers dive into my hair, fisting and releasing, brushing through the strands as she digs her fingernails into my scalp, sending me straight to heaven.

Before Sienna, I wouldn't have called myself an affectionate man.

Now I can't get enough of her touch.

"Want you," she murmurs against my lips. "Bedroom."

"Too far," I breathe and moan when she sinks her teeth into my earlobe and tugs. "Fucking hell, you make me crazy."

"Back at you, ace."

Chapter Twelve

~Sienna~

Holy Christ.

Maybe this wasn't a great idea because now I don't know how I'll ever come into my studio and *not* think about Quinn's hands all over my body.

He's making me crazy, in the best way possible.

And who knew that brush bristles felt like *that*? I didn't. And now I do.

And holy hell.

"Stop thinking," he mumbles against my neck just before he nibbles his way down to the top of my shoulder. "Just feel."

"Oh, I'm feeling," I reply. I can't resist plunging my fingers into his hair again. It's dark and thick, longer on top than the sides, and it feels like silk between my fingers.

He pins me against the wall, my hands above my head and

pressed to the wall above, as his mouth takes a journey down my neck, careful to avoid where he's painted me. I try to hitch my leg over his hip, but he won't stop moving.

"Just enjoy, sweetheart," he says.

"I'm squirmy." There's no other way to describe it. I can't stay still. I *need* to move against him.

Suddenly, he lifts me into his arms and carries me out of the bright studio to my kitchen, sets me on the island, spreads my legs, and squats before me.

"Whoa, change of venue," I mutter, getting my balance.

"I don't want you on the floor."

I frown down at him. "I'm already dirty."

"I don't want you on the floor," he repeats, voice firm. His hands are gliding up the inside of my thighs until his thumbs touch over my lips. "Do you have any idea how fucking beautiful you are?"

"You make me feel beautiful."

"You are," he replies, leaning in to press a kiss where my thigh meets my center. "You have a freckle right here."

"No, I don't."

He chuckles. "I'm looking at it, baby. You do. But not many anywhere else."

"Redhead without freckles," I agree and suck in a breath when he skims the tip of his tongue over the top of my shaved pussy. "God, Quinn."

"Mm, love hearing my name like that."

I lean back on my elbows, unwilling to take my eyes off

what he's doing down south. His hands are gentle. His mouth tender.

And my body is on fire.

He props my leg over his shoulder, and dives in for a long, deep kiss, and I'm lost under his spell. My back arches, and I'm pretty sure my whole body just exploded into a million twinkling lights.

When the world rushes back to me, Quinn is standing, unzipping his shorts, rolling on a condom, and pressing into me.

"Like a bloody vise," he growls, his jaw clenched shut. He buries his face in my neck and rides me like his life depends on it.

But he's not fucking me. No, we've done that before, and this isn't the same. It's not as hurried, as *trivial*.

Quinn is moving like he can't *not* claim me, and it's the most intoxicating sex I've ever had.

It's almost loving.

And God, I hope that's not just wishful thinking on my part, because I've fallen for this man, hook, line and sinker.

He links his fingers through mine and kisses my hand, then tucks our hands next to our bodies as he leans in, presses his lips to my mouth, and loses control spectacularly.

"YOU SHOULD STAY with me," Quinn says an hour later, after we've cleaned ourselves and the studio, and we're back to painting.

"Where?"

"At my condo," he says simply, loading his brush and watching me carefully as I fill in a building with dark gray.

"Why?"

"Because we're going to be working in Manhattan a lot over the next two weeks, and it'll be more convenient for you if you're nearby."

"Hmm." I nibble on the end of my brush, checking out my work, and thinking about Quinn's offer. Do I *want* to stay with him?

Duh. Of course I do. I love sleeping next to him, I love being *with* him.

"I don't know if that's a great idea."

"Why?" he asks calmly. It's like we're talking about where we want to eat for dinner, or the weather.

"Because we're working together, and if one of the law clerks found out—"

"Unless you tell them, they're not going to find out," he says. "I don't make it a habit to tell my employees about my personal relationships."

"Good point," I concede and clean my brush off. "I guess I'd better pack a bag."

His head whips over in surprise. "Really?"

"You were expecting more of a fight?"

"Well, yeah."

"I can give you one."

"No." He sets his brush down and takes my hand, practically pulling me down to my bedroom. "No, let's pack you a bag."

"Listen up," Quinn says Monday morning. We're in the larger of the conference rooms, with all the boxes lined against one wall, and the opposite wall empty for boxes as we finish going through them. "Sienna Hendricks is the opposing counsel on this case, and the owner of all these files. We have the same goal in mind: to find the truth. This case is different because it's a hundred years old. It's not a matter of a Google search, or looking through a computer for the files. We have to look by hand.

"Time is ticking, and that's why we've decided to move the operation here. With your help, this should go much faster. But Sienna's in charge."

"She's not a partner here," one of the clerks points out, his arms crossed over his chest. "I'm not comfortable taking orders from opposing counsel."

"Then you're welcome to go," Quinn says, pointing to the door.

"Great, I'll go back to my office."

"No, get your shit and leave. You're fired. This isn't up for discussion."

The man stares at Quinn in shock, then shrugs and stomps out.

"Does anyone else have an issue with this?" Quinn asks. The four remaining clerks all shake their heads.

"Tim's an idiot," a blond woman says, shaking her head. "This is fascinating."

"I agree," I reply with a smile and smooth my hands down my red suit. "My rules are actually very simple. I don't want you working on this if I'm not here. Like Quinn said, these are my family's personal files. However, I will be here all day, every day. This is my only priority until we wrap up the case."

"I'll be in and out," Quinn says, shoving his hands in his pockets. He's staring at me from across the room, and I swear, the sexual chemistry is so thick, you could cut it with a knife.

How can the others not feel it?

"But I'm just down the hall if there are questions. And with that, I'll leave you to it."

He nods and leaves, and I look around the room, grateful to have the help.

"Do you mind introducing yourselves?"

"I'm Christy," the blonde says with a smile. "This is Peter, Matt, and Caden."

"Great. Call me Sienna. We've already found these." I hold the receipts up for them to see. "There should be two more, but they could be anywhere in these boxes. I assume they'll look the same, but we don't know that for sure either."

"Needle in a haystack," Matt says with a sigh.

"Exactly," I agree. "I've also been pulling out marriage certificates, death certificates, things like that so they're not mixed in with the other nonsense. If you run across anything like that, I'd appreciate it if you just set it aside.

"But the receipts are the most important thing."

The door opens, and Quinn's assistant, Kami, walks in with a large pot of coffee.

"Quinn asked me to bring this in," she says with a smile. "There are mugs, sugar, creamer over here."

"Thanks, Kami," I reply with a grin. "Let's get to it."

An hour later, I glance up to see Caden pull a stack of papers out of a box, set them aside, and pull another stack out, then put it all back in the box and take it to the *finished* pile.

"You didn't look through those," I say.

"Yes, I did. They're just invoices from 1943."

"I'm sorry, maybe I didn't make myself clear. You have to look between every paper. The files aren't organized well."

"Are you kidding?" Caden asks.

"Unfortunately, no. I know, pain in the ass, but that's why we need your help."

"Jesus," he mutters, retrieves the box, and starts combing through it, one paper at a time.

Kami returns with a tray of fruit and what looks like packets of trail mix.

"More snacks," she says with a grin, sets them on the wet bar, and sees herself out.

"We never get snacks around here," Peter says.

"Special guest," Christy reminds him, pointing at me, and I feel my cheeks flush. "Maybe Quinn has a crush on you."

"Or maybe he's just being kind to a colleague," I reply with a laugh. "And are you guys saying that you work under harsh conditions most of the time?"

"No," Christy says immediately. "I've worked for far worse than this. They just don't usually offer us refreshments."

"But I'll take them," Caden adds as he pops a handful of trail mix in his mouth and munches loudly.

The rest of the morning is smooth and quiet, if uneventful. We don't find any more receipts of payment for the borrowed money.

"You guys should go get some lunch," I say at last and rub my neck. "Give your eyes a break."

"Good idea," Peter says. "Want us to bring you back anything?"

"No, but thanks for asking."

The four of them leave, and five minutes later, Quinn walks in carrying a bag and wearing a smile.

He locks the door behind him, making me giggle.

"Alone at last," he says. He sets the food on the table, then sweeps me up in a long, wet kiss. "How was your morning?"

"Fine. Uneventful. But we've already made a lot more headway than you and I do alone."

"That's the goal," he says with a nod.

"Also, you sent me trail mix."

"You need protein," he replies with a stern face. "I don't want you to go hungry."

"Christy thinks you might have a crush on me."

"Christy would be right." His hand slides down my back to my ass and he yanks me against him, buries his face in my neck, and nibbles me there. "You're delicious."

"You know, we're at work."

"The door's locked and no one gives a shit."

I giggle and give in. I *want* him to kiss me.

And he does. Boy, does he.

When we finally come up for air, I have to pull away, smooth my hand over my hair, and take a deep breath.

"You'd better give me that food before I do something silly like strip out of my clothes and lie on this table."

His brown eyes flare with lust and humor.

"Let's do that."

"No." I laugh and reach for the bag of food. "Maybe later."

"Definitely later."

"You need to sleep," Quinn says. It's late, after ten in the evening, and I haven't gone back to his place for the night yet.

"I just want to finish this. I want to find it."

"You're exhausted, sweetheart. You need to rest, and get back to it in the morning."

I yawn, and then shrug. "I guess you're right."

My phone starts to ring, making me frown.

"Who's calling at this time of night? You're with me." I read the display and answer. "Uncle Patrick?"

"Where are the boxes?" he demands.

"What boxes?"

"You know what boxes. The files. They're not here."

I look up at Quinn, whose face is like stone.

"Why are you at Grandpa's?"

"I own this house now, Sienna, I have every right to be here. I also have every right to know where my father's property is."

"It's in my custody," I reply, standing so I can pace the room. "And I'm going to be honest, I don't appreciate you calling at this time of night to grill me about this. You know I would never do anything to harm Grandpa's things, and I'm working on an open case on behalf of our family."

"You're right," he says with a sigh. "I came here to sit for a while. I sometimes do that late at night when I can't sleep. I miss him."

"I miss him too, but Uncle Patrick, you crossed a line."

"I disagree," he replies, his voice hard again. "I'd appreciate an answer."

"Like I said, it's in my custody, and I'm working the case full-time, until it's done. Everything will be returned when the case is over."

Quinn begins to knead my shoulders from behind and I lean into his touch, immediately calming.

Uncle Patrick hangs up without saying good-bye, and I sigh, then lean back when Quinn wraps his arms around me, hugging me from behind.

"That was weird."

"He's angry?" Quinn asks.

"Yeah, I guess he went to Grandpa's and is pissed that the boxes are gone. It's so weird, it's as if he doesn't think I can handle this case. This isn't the first time he's called me out on something regarding it."

"Maybe he's worried," Quinn suggests, but his voice doesn't sound sure.

"I don't know, he's never questioned me before."

"Hmm."

I turn in his arms and frown up at him. "What?"

"I don't know him well, but there's just something about him that I don't trust."

"Don't be silly." I shake my head and pull away, gathering my files and briefcase. "Uncle Patrick is just going through some grief, or loneliness. Or maybe he's worried that the park will be lost because of this. It's been a staple of the neighborhood for a very long time, and it's something that my family has always been proud of."

"Maybe," Quinn says with a thin smile.

"But you don't think so."

"Like I said, I don't know him," he replies and takes my hand to walk with me down to the car. "But I don't like that he upset you."

"I'll be fine. Nothing that some sleep won't fix." I lean against him in the elevator, kiss his chest through his shirt. "It was a good idea to have me stay with you. It *is* easier."

"I do have good ideas once in a while," he says with a smile. "Do I need to carry you to the car?"

"No, I think I can walk."

But I feel dead on my feet. The longer we go without finding our proof, the more exhausting it is.

I'm worried.

BEFORE LONG, WE'RE in Quinn's condo, and I'm sitting at the end of his long, gray sofa, my legs pulled up under me, with a steaming mug of tea in my hands.

I'm staring at the ocean painting I gave him.

It really does suit him and this space.

"You haven't even changed," Quinn says as he joins me, taking my mug out of my hands so he can take a sip. He's in some gym shorts and nothing else.

God, that V at his hips is something to write home about.

"How do you find time to go to the gym?" I ask him.

"I usually go early in the morning before I go to the office," he says and passes me back the mug. "But lately—"

"You've been with me."

I sip the tea and feel guilt set up residence in my belly.

"I've taken up a lot of your time."

"I'm not complaining."

"I know." I reach for his hand, threading our fingers. "But I feel bad. I'm taking time from your business *and* your life. I've even imposed in your condo for the immediate future."

"What's with this mood tonight, sweetheart?" He wraps one arm around my shoulders and tucks me against him, buries his lips and nose in my hair, and kisses me gently. "I told you before, I rarely do anything that I don't want to. Besides, who needs the gym when I'm getting a regular workout with you?"

I chuckle and squeeze his fingers.

"True. I'm just saying, if it's too much, just tell me. It won't hurt my feelings."

Much.

Okay, it will.

"Being with you is never enough, Sienna. I love every minute. So stop thinking like this and enjoy your tea before I carry you to my bed to have my way with you."

"That sounds promising."

Chapter Thirteen

~Sienna~

"You didn't sleep well," Quinn says quietly. We're in his car, driving into the office. We don't always drive in, since his office and home are so close, but he said he has errands to run later. We just left Starbucks, and I'm sipping gratefully at my second cup this morning. "Was it my bed?"

"No, your bed is comfortable. It's my brain." I sigh, watching as the city is coming to life. It's before seven, so rush hour hasn't hit in full force quite yet, but there are plenty of people bustling about. "I can't turn it off. I don't know, Quinn, maybe I should go home. I know it's easier to stay at your place, but I might be able to unwind better there."

He takes my hand in his and kisses it. "Today will be better, sweetheart."

"I hope so."

"I hate that you feel this way, Sienna. If you have another rough night tonight, I'll help you move your things back home."

I nod, a pit forming in my throat. I really *enjoy* spending time with him at his place. But I miss my studio. I would have painted for a few hours last night, and it would have relaxed me enough to go to sleep.

"But I'll be bringing some things with me too," he says, surprising me.

"You'd come stay with me?"

"Absolutely."

"But that doesn't make sense."

"Being with you makes perfect sense," he says, kisses my hand again, and then turns into the underground parking for his building.

I don't know how to reply to that, so I don't.

When we walk onto the floor of his office, Kami is already at her desk. She glances up with a smile.

"Good morning," she says. If she thinks it's odd that we've arrived together, she doesn't let on. "You have a few messages on your desk, Quinn. And you don't have anything on your calendar until this afternoon."

"Perfect," he replies. "I will need to see you in my office in thirty minutes."

"Yes, sir."

He walks with me to the conference room, unlocks it for me, and once we're inside, he locks it again.

"I'm going to be out of the office this morning," he says with a sigh. "I have to take Mom to an appointment."

"Is she okay?" I ask, immediately kicking myself for not asking about her earlier. "Is she having more memory problems?"

"Yeah, and she forgot to tell her doctor about it last week, like I figured she would. So I'm going with her today. But I'll be in this afternoon, and if you need anything, I'm only a phone call away."

"Quinn." I walk to him and frame his face in my hands. "I was an attorney before I met you. I'll be just fine. Go take care of your mama."

"You're pretty wonderful," he replies with a smile and leans down to press his lips to my forehead. "You know that, right?"

"I'm damn amazing," I say with a chuckle. "And thanks for trying to make me feel better. I'm in a funk. I think I'm afraid that we won't find what we're looking for before we head back to court."

"We'll find it."

"Whose side are you on?" I ask playfully.

"The truth," he says simply. "And I'm also on the side of making sure that you're okay."

"Thank you," I repeat just as his lips cover mine.

"I have to go talk to Kami for a moment, and then I have to go get Mom."

"Did you even *really* need to come to the office this morning?"

"Yes, I had to bring you here."

"I could have walked myself."

He grins as he pulls away, that self-assured, cocky grin that does things to my lady bits. "But then I wouldn't have been able to spend the morning with you, and that would have been a pity."

"Go on, charmer. Have a good morning."

He waves and leaves, and I get settled in what I've come to think of as my usual spot at the end of the table. I drain my coffee cup and toss it in the wastebasket, then open the box that I'd started on last night.

At eight, Christy, Peter, Caden, and Matt filter in, carrying coffees, and immediately dive into their boxes.

It's almost lunchtime when Peter suddenly stands and thrusts a paper in the air.

"I found something!"

I rush over to join him, take the paper from his hands, and feel my face break out in an excited smile.

"You did it," I say and give him a high five. "This one is dated six months after the last."

"She wasn't kidding yesterday," Peter tells the others. "I literally found this in a box of grocery receipts."

"They kept *everything*," Christy says in exasperation. "I mean, it's cool to see what the price of eggs was back then, but why would they save it?"

"I have no idea," I reply honestly as I tuck the third receipt in its folder with the others. "It's completely frustrating and fascinating, all at the same time. I'll probably eventually pull out everything that's important and shred or burn the rest."

"That seems kind of sad," Matt replies with a frown.

"Are you sentimental?" I ask him with a grin.

"I mean, some of these things are a hundred years old. Maybe there are museums that would like to get their hands on some of it, just because it *is* interesting."

"That's a good point." I tap my finger on my lips. "Maybe I'll look into that. You're right, it would seem like a waste to just throw it all away."

"I'm starving," Caden says. "Since we've found something useful, what do you say we take an early lunch?"

"Great idea," I reply with a grin. "Can you guys just bring me back something? I'm going to check in with my office and work on a couple of things here."

"Sure thing," Christy says with a wave as they file out, a bounce in their step from the encouragement of finding the receipt.

Hell, *I* want to turn a cartwheel.

Not that I ever could.

I take my phone out of my handbag to call the office, but it starts to ring in my hand.

"Hello?"

"Hello, darling," Mom says brightly. "Am I interrupting?"

No, it's just the middle of the workday. What would you be interrupting?

But I just smile. "Nope, what's up?"

"Well, I've decided to have a family dinner on Sunday. I haven't seen you in quite a while."

"I know." The daughter guilt sets in. "I'm sorry, I've just been busy with the park case, and keeping up with other work stuff."

"I understand, but I hope you can take a couple of hours on Sunday to spend some time with your family."

"I'll be working with Quinn early in the day."

"Well, bring him," she says, a little too brightly. "Your sister has told me a lot about him already, and I'd like to meet the man that you're dating."

I roll my eyes and make a mental note to have a talk with Lou.

"There's not been a lot of time for dating, Mom."

"Bring him anyway," she says. "I insist."

"Okay, I'll let him know that he's invited. I'm not making any promises."

"Great, we'll see you two on Sunday, then. Let's say six?"

"Six it is."

I hang up and laugh, shaking my head. My mom's never been good at taking no for an answer, especially from her kids.

She and Quinn should get along great.

"How DID IT go today?" I ask Quinn as he walks into the conference room. It's past six. The others left a while ago, after I insisted that it was okay.

"The doctor thinks the memory stuff is from her medication," he says as he lowers himself into the chair next to me and rubs his face with his hand. He looks tired. Worried.

So I reach over for his hand, giving it a squeeze.

He pulls me out of my seat and into his lap, lays his cheek between my breasts, and takes a deep breath.

"That's good, though, right?"

"It's definitely better than it being a brain issue," he agrees and pats my ass. "They're making some adjustments, and we'll see how she feels."

"Well, that has to be a relief." I kiss his head and run my fingers through his hair. "I have good news too."

"Tell me."

"We found another receipt."

He looks up, his eyes wide with happiness. "That's awesome."

"I know. We can now account for three-quarters of the loan, and that makes me *very* happy."

"I'm so glad." He kisses my neck.

"Part of me thinks that this should be enough proof to go to the judge with."

"I would agree if it was just about anyone other than Judge Maxton," he says. "She's a stickler."

"And I wouldn't be happy with anything less than finding that last receipt," I agree. "So we'll keep plugging along."

"That we will." He kisses me again, then nudges me off his lap. "Now, let's go home."

"Quinn, it's only six. I'd like to get a couple more hours of work in."

"I forbid it."

I cock a brow, brace my hand on his hip, and tip my head to the side.

"Excuse me?"

His lips twitch with humor. "That didn't work? Fine. You've been working your ass off. You found more of what you need today, and you're exhausted. Let me take you home, feed you, and you can get some rest before diving back in tomorrow."

"That's better." I shake my head as I gather my things to leave for the day. "You've gotta know me well enough by now to know that if you *forbid* anything, I'm going to do exactly that."

"I mostly wanted to see the look on your gorgeous face when I said it," he says with a smug smile. "I wasn't disappointed. It's the same face you have in court, and it makes me hard as fuck."

That stops me in my tracks. "Really?"

"Oh yeah. Don't forget, I'm a courtroom junkie, and you're damn hot in the courtroom."

"You've only seen me in action once."

"And that was plenty for me to know."

I laugh and lead him out of the conference room, waiting while he closes and locks the door, then follow him down to his car.

"You seem to be feeling better tonight."

He's pulled out of the garage and we're headed to his place, which isn't far.

"I am," I agree. "It helps that we found that money. I guess it gave me some of the energy and confidence that slipped yesterday."

"I'm glad."

The ride up to his condo is quiet. He opens the door, and for the second time in the span of minutes, I'm stopped in my tracks.

"Holy shit, Quinn."

There's a fire in the fireplace, and lit candles all over the room. There must be five dozen red roses in vases on the kitchen island.

But the best part?

The Chinese takeout sitting on the coffee table, in front of the fire, and the red rose petals sprinkled all over the floor.

"I told you I wanted to feed you."

"This is just so *beautiful*." I set my bag down, kick out of my shoes, and gaze around. "It's also a horrible fire hazard. I hope it hasn't been like this for long."

Quinn laughs as he kicks off his own shoes, sheds his jacket, and rolls his sleeves up, getting comfortable. "Kami just left five minutes ago."

"Quinn, is it smart that she knows what's happening between us?"

"Kami's worked for me for almost five years. She's discreet, and loyal, and I know without a doubt that anything I tell her stays between the two of us."

I take a deep breath, and then nod. "Okay, if you trust her, I do too."

"I got you Kung Pao chicken," he says, holding up the box.

"And I love that it's a picnic." I sit on the floor next to him and dig into the food. It smells delicious. "This is supercozy. Was it her idea or yours?"

"I can't believe you just asked that." His voice is calm as he digs into his lo mein. "It was *my* idea, sassy girl."

"It was a good one." We munch on our food, leaning in for quick kisses between bites. "I don't think I've ever had a fire in the summer before."

"Air-conditioning is a godsend in moments like this," he says with a satisfied smile. "Are you going to eat that last egg roll?"

"No, I'm full. Go ahead."

He eats it in two bites, wipes his mouth, and then reaches for his jacket and pulls a little blue box out of the pocket.

"This is for you."

I stare at it for a moment and then slowly shake my head. "You've already done a lot with the flowers and the fire. The food. You don't have to give me presents, Quinn."

"You don't want it?" He cocks an eyebrow, and just when he's going to pull it away, I snatch it out of his hand, making him laugh.

"Of course I want it, crazy man. I'm just saying you didn't have to."

I pull the white ribbon loose, and nestled inside is a blue pouch. I pull the strings loose, tip it over, and a necklace slides onto my palm, with a gold key on the chain.

"This is gorgeous."

"The key is because—"

"If you say it's because it's the key to your heart, I will walk right out that door. That's way too cheesy."

He tips his head back and laughs. He's still chuckling when he helps me fasten it around my neck.

"No, I was going to say I thought it was pretty, and that it would suit you. But now whenever anyone asks, I'm going to tell them that I got it for you because you hold the key to my heart."

"You're so cheesy," I grumble, wrinkling my nose, and earn a tickle in the ribs from Quinn. "No fair. I'm defenseless when you tickle me."

"Good," he says, but his touch is lighter as he drags his fingers up my side, and into my hair, pulling it loose from the pins. It spills over his hands as he shakes it out, and rubs his fingertips over my scalp.

"Oh, that's nice."

"I love your hair," he says. "It's so soft and the color is amazing. Why do you always wear it up?"

"It's part of my armor." The words are out before I realize it, and he's frowning down at me.

"Why do you need armor?"

"Because I'm a female attorney," I say at last. "And I need to be taken seriously. So I wear stuffy suits, and I keep my hair pulled up, and while I'm not afraid to look feminine, I am a firm believer in being professional."

"What about when you're not at work?"

"It's just habit, and it keeps it out of my way."

He watches his fingers as he pulls them through the strands.

"Can I request that you wear it down once in a while, when it's just us?"

"Of course you can." I kiss his wrist. "I'll do that."

His eyes are hot on mine as he leans in to kiss me, gently, softly, taking this moment from playful to sexy in the blink of an eye.

My fingers are already unfastening the buttons of his shirt, anxious to get to his warm skin. He doesn't even bother unbuttoning my shirt, he strips it over my head, leaving me in a white bra and my skirt.

"I always think that I'm going to take it slow with you." His voice is thicker now, full of lust and yearning. "But once I get my hands on your skin, I can't hold myself back. It's like it's a race to be buried inside of you, to hear you as you come apart."

"It's not a race," I whisper. "It's not a race at all."

Our clothes peel away, piece by piece, until it's just Quinn and me, in front of this fire, on a plush area rug and rose petals.

I push him onto his back and kneel next to him, enjoying the way the light dances along his skin.

"I want to paint you," I say with a soft smile. "Like this. With the flames dancing on your body, and the way you're looking at me right now."

"You can paint me whenever you like." His hand is dragging up and down my thigh, over my ass, sending goose bumps over my skin. I take my time memorizing him with my hands, and then my tongue gets in on the action, and Quinn's hand moves from my thigh to my hair, fisting and holding on tightly.

"You taste good." I lick him from balls to tip, then sink over him and take him for the ride of his life.

"Fucking hell," he growls. He's not pressing on my head, but rather just holding on, letting me lick and suck him.

Letting me enjoy him.

Until I can't stand it anymore and I climb over him, sinking over him.

With my hands planted on his chest, I ride him. Slowly at first, but then I can't stand it, I need to pick up the pace.

And he's happy to oblige.

He cups my ass and guides me up and down, until we're both squirming with absolute rapture.

He sits up, kisses me firmly, his arms wrapped around me and the shift in angle sends me straight into the stars. I cry out, his name muffled against his lips.

"Yes," he says, panting hard. "That's it, baby."

We're spent, sitting here, staring into each other's eyes. Quinn kisses my lips, my neck, my shoulder, then lifts me off him and disappears into the guest bathroom.

He returns with a wet cloth and cleans us both up, then urges me to my feet.

"I have one more thing to show you."

"Quinn, I—"

"No arguments this time." He passes me a throw blanket, which I wrap around me, holding it in a knot at my breasts, and follow him down the hall to the spare bedroom.

But when he opens the door, the bed and dresser are gone.

In their places are an easel, blank canvases, a table with paints and brushes, and a tarp on the floor.

I spin, staring at him with wide eyes and absolute shock.

"What did you do?"

"I built a pool," he says dryly, turning around to see the room again. He wraps his arms around my middle, hugging me from behind and kisses my cheek. "Kami and Louise helped."

"These paints are badass. I don't buy them for myself because they're too expensive."

"I know." He kisses the ball of my shoulder. "Louise told me."

"Why did you do this?"

He sighs, then walks around to face me and frames my face in his hands the way I did to him earlier.

"I did it because you need this. It soothes you, and I want you to feel at home here, Sienna. I'm so in love with you that I ache with it. I want you to stay, for as long as you're willing to. I don't want you to feel that you aren't comfortable here with me."

I'm blinking, soaking in everything he's saying, and fighting the urge to pinch myself, just to make sure that I'm not dreaming.

"Oh my."

My fingers find the key at my neck and fiddle with it. My God, he has the key to *my* heart.

"Are you okay?" he asks gently.

"I love you too," I blurt out, looking up through my eyelashes, suddenly feeling shy. "And I'm just so grateful, Quinn. Truly."

He tugs me into a fierce hug, and when he pulls away, I hurry around him to his bedroom.

"Where are you going?"

"I need clothes. I have some painting to do!"

Chapter Fourteen

~Quinn~

*G*od, I hate that guy," Carter mutters as we jog down the steps of the courthouse, headed back to our office after a morning of courtroom work. "He's *such* a prick."

"And your client," I remind him with a laugh, patting him on the shoulder. "You handled him great. Not taking any shit is the way to go, every time."

"There's no other way to go, and the fucker can fire me if he doesn't like it," he grumbles as we climb into his car to drive back to the office. Before he starts the car, he checks his phone and scowls. "Jesus, this has been blowing up. The school *and* Nora."

Nora is Carter's assistant and has been with him for many years. She's been a huge help to him since Darcy died, especially where Gabby's concerned.

With the phone piped through the Bluetooth system of the car, I can hear the messages as they play.

"Hello, Mr. Shaw, this is Judy at Gabby's school. She's in my office and I need to talk to you as soon as possible."

"Shit," Carter mutters as the next message plays.

"It's Nora. The school called, and they want to see you. I know you're in court, so I'm headed there now."

"Thank God for Nora," I say.

"There are two more messages," Carter replies.

"Me again," Nora says, her voice more hurried. "I have Gabby. Will tell you more when I see you, but she's not hurt."

"I guess that's good news," he murmurs.

"Hey," Nora says through the speakers, "we're back at the office. See you soon."

"When did all this happen?" I ask as we pull into the garage.

"More than an hour ago," he replies. We hurry up to the office, and I stick with him as he walks briskly to his own office. Nora is sitting at her desk just outside of Carter's office door.

"The preteen drama queen is in your office," Nora says with a grin. "She's been suspended until Monday, and I already have her phone in my desk. But Carter."

He stops and looks down at the pretty blond woman. I see the look in his eyes. I'm not blind or stupid.

He has the hots for Nora.

But my guess would be that he doesn't want to blur the lines between personal and professional, which I totally understand.

"You really need to listen to her before you fly off the handle."

"I don't fly off the handle," Carter replies, to which Nora just rolls her eyes.

"Of course. You're completely calm at all times."

"Thanks for taking care of things, Nora," Carter says as he walks to his door, then turns to me. "You don't have to be here for this."

"Oh yeah, I do." I smile widely. "I don't have anything more pressing to do, and I want to know what's going on."

"Fine." Carter marches into his office, and there's Gabby, sitting in her father's chair, her arms crossed over her chest, and a scowl on her pretty little face.

"Hey, munchkin," Carter says. She doesn't look up from whatever she's glaring at on Carter's desk.

"Hi."

We both sit across from her, as if *we're* the ones who have been called into the principal's office.

"Wanna talk about it?" I ask.

Gabby shakes her head. "No. It doesn't matter."

"Pretty sure it matters," Carter replies. "Since you've been suspended and all, sounds like it definitely matters."

"No, it doesn't," she says, her eyes spitting anger as she turns them to her father. "I didn't even do anything wrong, and I got kicked out of school. I don't want to go back. I just want to be homeschooled."

"You know that isn't possible," Carter replies, and I'm happy that he *does* sound perfectly calm and reasonable. "Gabby, explain what happened, and maybe we can help."

She chews on her lip, then sighs and leans her head back on the chair.

"There's this girl named Lily at school, and she's not really very pretty, but that's not a big deal because she's super nice and really funny."

I can already tell where this is going.

"I like her, and I always invite her to have lunch with us even though Claire can sometimes be a witch, except with the B instead of the W."

"Yes, I'm following you," Carter says dryly.

"So Claire is the B-word," Gabby reiterates and I have to hide my smile behind my hand. Gabby's trying to grow up so quickly, and she's just *dying* to curse. "And we're sitting at lunch, and everything is totally fine. We were talking about this new movie on Netflix, and how the guy is cute, and Lily said she thought he was *so* cute, and then Claire rolled her eyes and told Lily that a hot guy like that would never be interested in someone as ugly as her."

Gabby's eyes well with tears, and my smile is immediately gone.

"Claire does sound like a bitch," I whisper, and Carter frowns at me, giving me the silent, universal signal that says *don't egg her on.*

"She is," Gabby agrees. "And she's just plain mean. I mean, why does she have to say stuff like that?"

"So what did you do?" Carter asks, and now Gabby chews her lip again and shrugs one shoulder.

"Nothing."

"No way," Carter replies, sitting forward in his chair. "They didn't suspend you for glaring at Claire the B."

"Well, I was sitting next to her, across from Lily, and I sort of—"

We wait, literally on the edge of our seats, for her to continue, but now she's gone all shy.

"Tell me you kicked her bratty little ass," I say, earning another glare from Carter.

"I threw applesauce in her face," Gabby says. "And then she pulled my hair, so I might have pulled her earring out of her ear."

Jesus. Gabby's a scrapper.

"You *might have*?" Carter asks incredulously. "Jesus, Gabby, you made her bleed."

"She deserved it," Gabby replies with big crocodile tears rolling down her cheeks. "She was so *mean*, and this isn't the first time. I just couldn't stand it anymore. Lily didn't deserve it. She didn't say anything bad to Claire."

"Good girl," I whisper, but she doesn't hear me as she sniffles through her tears.

"But I'm the one who got punished because Claire lied and said she didn't do anything to me first."

"And they believed that?" I ask.

"It was my word against hers, and she was the one bleeding."

God, she sounds so grown up right now. Where is the chubby toddler that I swear she was just four minutes ago?

"Violence isn't the way to handle the situation," Carter says, sitting back in his chair. "And you *will* apologize for hurting her."

"Dad!"

"I'm not finished speaking."

She closes her lips, frowning again.

"I am proud of you for standing up for your friend. Being loyal is an excellent trait, and I want you to always do that. But the answer isn't to act out physically."

"What was I supposed to do?" she demands.

"Walk away," Carter suggests. "Tell Claire that she's mean and you don't want to be her friend, gather your lunches, and go sit somewhere else."

"She would just laugh at us," Gabby murmurs.

"Let her laugh," I say. "Seriously, who cares what Claire the B thinks? Let her laugh, but you won't have to sit with her anymore, and you'll be with your *true* friend."

"On Monday, you *will* apologize to Claire. Let's hope that Claire tells her parents the truth, and that we don't get sued for any medical bills that come out of this."

"They can't do that," Gabby says.

"Yes, they can," Carter and I say at the same time.

"And if they do," I continue, "we'll deal with it. Because just like you have Lily's back, we have your back."

Gabby nods. "Since I was helping a friend, can I have my phone back?"

"On Monday," Carter replies. "You're suspended from that for now too."

"This sucks," she grumbles.

"We're going home early today," Carter says as I stand to go to my own office now. "What do you have tomorrow?"

"Tomorrow's Friday," I murmur, thinking. "I have my meeting with Bruce in the morning, and then I think Sienna and I are having dinner with Finn and London tomorrow evening. You should join us."

And bring Nora.

"Not this time," Carter says, shaking his head. "I'll see you tomorrow."

I walk down toward my office, pausing at the conference room that Sienna's working in. The door is open, and Matt is leaning over Sienna's shoulder, reading.

His hand is on her.

And that doesn't fly with me.

"How's it going in here?" I ask, leaning against the doorjamb.

"I found a journal," Sienna says with a smile. "This is my great-grandmother's journal from when she was dating my great-grandfather."

"And it's explicit," Matt adds with a grin. "Great-Grandpa was a bit of a freak."

Sienna laughs, but my eyes are pinned to Matt's hand on Sienna's arm, which he immediately moves away.

"I think it's time for lunch," I announce, and all four of the clerks stand, ready to get something to eat.

"See you in a bit," Christy says to Sienna. "Do you want anything?"

"No, I'm good. Thanks."

They leave and I close the door, then lock it.

"Seriously, this woman should have written romance novels," Sienna says, still reading the book in her hands. "She was way before her time. She could have given *Fifty Shades* a run for its money."

"He was touching you," I say, sitting next to her. She looks up with a frown, confusion on her face.

"Who was?"

"Matt."

She blinks quickly. "When?"

"Just now." I rub my hands over my face, pissed at myself for being jealous, but unable to stop it. "And I didn't like it."

"We were reading this journal," she says, holding it up to show me. "We were laughing, and he touched me."

"And he didn't take his hand away until I gave him the stink eye."

Sienna closes the book and sits back in her chair, watching me. "You're jealous."

"Fuck yes, I am."

"Quinn, you have no reason to be jealous."

"Doesn't make it any less of a thing."

She sighs and moves from her chair to my lap, wrapping her arms around my neck and kissing me long and deep.

"Trust me when I say, I have *zero* urge to do that to Matt."

"I'd kill him otherwise."

"You're awfully violent."

"When it comes to you? Yes." I kiss her again, but my muscles are relaxing now. "I won't apologize for feeling territorial. That's what being in love with you does to me."

She smiles, her whole face lighting up. "I don't mind. Just don't beat anyone up."

"I'm not Gabby."

She tilts her head in confusion, and I tell her all about my niece's suspension from school.

"She was doing what she thought was right," Sienna says. "And that Claire sounds like a bitch."

I laugh and hug her close. "That's what Gabby calls her. *Claire the B.*"

"Good name for her. I got a call from my mom the other day and forgot to tell you. She invited us to dinner on Sunday."

"Both of us?"

She nods and bites her lip. "Seems Lou told her we're dating."

"What time?"

"Six. But you don't have to go if you don't want to."

"Of course I want to. And as much as I want to stay here with you all day, I have to go to my office for a while. I have my weekly meeting with Bruce House tomorrow morning and I need to prepare."

"Is he coming here?" she asks.

"Yes."

"Can I speak to him?"

"What would you like to say?"

"I want to ask him to drop the case," she says with a shrug. "I know it's a long shot, but I want to try."

"I'll arrange for the meeting."

"THIS IS UNEXPECTED," Bruce says the next morning when I show Sienna into my office.

"I asked Quinn if I could have a minute of your time," she begins and sits at the table across from him. "I wanted to update you. I've found three-quarters of the money that was loaned. I have receipts with the same handwriting of the letter in your possession that say the money was paid back."

"But not all of it," Bruce says.

"No." Sienna crosses her hands over her folder, not looking away from Bruce. "But we still have a lot of boxes to look through, and I'm confident that we will find it. Because of this, I'd like to ask you to drop the case."

Bruce looks to me, but I don't say anything, waiting for his response. I *want* him to drop the case. I also want him to tell her that it's her uncle who gave him the letter in the first place, so Sienna is no longer in the dark, and I don't feel like a massive douchebag for keeping it from her.

I'm sorely disappointed.

"I'm not dropping the case," Bruce says, and before Sienna can reply, he holds his hand up. "I'm not trying to be a jerk here. I'm a businessman, plain and simple. You have proof that part of the money was paid back."

"*Most* of the money."

"But not all of it. Which means that at this moment, I still own it."

"What do you want?" Sienna asks. "I'll gladly pay you the five thousand dollars right now."

"We both know that it's worth much more than that."

"That was the loan amount," she counters, but then nods. "Okay, I'll pay you twenty-five thousand."

"Five million," Bruce replies, and Sienna's eyes widen, her jaw clenches, and she drops her fisted hands under the table in her lap.

"Bruce, it might be best to settle out of court. We don't know that the judge would rule in your favor, especially given that the majority of the money has been found. It's likely that the rest was paid as well."

"Yet, if the proof of that isn't found, I still legally own it," he counters. "Like I said, I'm a businessman, and I know what that property is worth. I'm not willing to give up on it. We have more than a week until court, so that gives you time to find the rest of your proof."

Sienna sighs, then nods and stands to walk out of the room. But before she can shut the door, Bruce calls her back.

"Good luck to you, Miss Hendricks."

Her eyes flick to mine, and then she shuts the door behind her.

"She's a beautiful woman," Bruce says casually. "I wonder if I signed the property over to her if she'd go to bed with me."

"I wonder if you could find another attorney who would

take you on in time for the court date," I reply, my blood boiling over. I want to punch him in his smarmy face. I want to have him thrown out of my building.

But until this case is finished, I won't sever ties.

The moment the gavel falls, however, Bruce will need to find new counsel. I don't care how much money I make from him.

He glances at me in surprise. "You're interested in her." He sits back, his hands steepled in front of him, thinking. His eyes are too full of mirth for my liking. "I hope that interest won't influence you in how you handle this case."

"I dislike men who are disrespectful to women, especially in professional settings," I say as I stand. "I'll see you next week."

Bruce doesn't put up a fight as he leaves my office. I send a text to Finn and Carter.

> We'll no longer be working with Bruce when this case is done.

It's for the best.

"It's BEEN A crazy week," Sienna says as we join Finn and London for dinner later in the evening at my condo. Sienna is cooking, and the condo smells amazing.

"Tell me about it," London says with a nod as Sienna sets a tray of bread in the oven. "I think we're all a little stressed right now, but I have something to talk about to take our minds off the tough stuff."

"What's that?" Sienna asks. I pour her a glass of wine and she kisses my bicep in thanks.

"You guys are seriously so cute together. Okay, engagement party," London replies with an excited little shimmy. "We need to plan."

"*We* do?" I ask.

"Yes," London says with a nod. "I need your input. I don't want it to get too out of hand. Quinn planned Finn's fortieth birthday party last year, and it was *so* great."

"Aside from how you almost got killed that night, it was a great party," I agree.

"Wait. You almost got *killed*?"

"That's a different story for another day," London says, shaking her head. "My point is, Quinn is good at this, and I want his input. And yours, Sienna."

"Hire a party planner," I suggest. "They can handle all the details and take it off your plate."

"I thought of that." London nods. "And I will absolutely do that for the wedding, but I want this party to be more intimate."

"I can help," Sienna announces, wiping her hands on the towel that she's thrown over her shoulder. She looks fucking amazing in my kitchen. "Actually, Louise can. My sister throws an awesome party. And I'm not talking your run-of-the-mill birthday party. I'll show you photos."

She takes out her phone and shows us all photos of some of the parties Louise has thrown.

"These are gorgeous," London breathes. "Does she do this for a living?"

"No, but she should. And I know if you asked, you could hire her to help you."

"I'll take her number right now," London says. "Thank you so much."

"Of course." Sienna glances at Finn, who's remained quiet during the whole exchange. "What do you think of all this?"

"She can have whatever she wants. Big party, little party, *no* party. As long as she marries me, I don't give a fuck."

"That might be the sweetest thing I've ever heard," Sienna says with a sigh.

"Sweeter than the reason I gave you that necklace?" I ask, enjoying the way her eyes narrow on me.

"What's the reason?" London asks.

"Nothing," Sienna says, shaking her head. "It's an inside joke."

"They have inside jokes already," London says to Finn as she elbows him in the gut. "See? It's going well."

"It's going great," I reply as I sip my wine, my eyes still pinned to the stunning woman bouncing around my kitchen as if she owns the place.

I never thought I'd agree with my brother about this, but I feel the same way. She can have whatever she wants as long as she's mine.

Chapter Fifteen

~Sienna~

I want to do something for Quinn. It's early Saturday morning, and I'm standing in my new studio in Quinn's condo, cleaning my brushes.

My man was still sleeping soundly when I woke, and I didn't want to disturb him, so I came in here, and it's *marvelous*.

He was absolutely right. I needed this to feel at home here, and he gave it to me. So in return, I want to do something for him today.

With the help of the law clerks, we've made a ton of progress in working our way through the boxes of documents. We can take one day off to just be.

I have this, the studio, to calm me. But Quinn needs something different, and I'm determined to give it to him. We've been racing and zip lining. I know he'd be up for either of those again today, but I kind of want to do something different.

Something unexpected.

I bite my lip and stow my brushes and paints, then head for the shower.

If I'm not mistaken, there was a movie years ago with Will Smith and Eva Mendes, and they went jet skiing in New York Harbor. I wonder if that's a thing? I bet Quinn would love it.

I reach for my phone and Google search jet skiing in New York Harbor, and sure enough, it's a thing. I quickly make reservations for us, and after my shower, I walk into the bedroom to find that Quinn is already awake. His arms are crossed behind his head in the bed, and he's watching me with happy blue eyes.

"You look ready to tackle the day," he says with a grin.

"I've been up for a while," I reply and sit on the bed at his hip. "I think we should play hooky today."

He cocks a brow. "*You* want to play hooky? Miss Responsible?"

"I know, it's a new thing for me." I lean in and press a kiss to his lips. "I have a surprise for you."

"Do you?" His hands skim up and down my arms. "Do we have time for a tumble in my bed first?"

"No." I rub my nose against his, then hurry to start getting dressed. "And you'll need to bring swim trunks and a change of clothes."

"You're quite mysterious this morning."

I send him a grin as I throw clothes into a tote bag, thankful that I threw a bathing suit in with my things when I moved in with him last week.

"Hurry up," I say as I rush out of his bedroom. "Oh, and I'm driving."

I can hear him laughing as I grab us each a bottle of water, and my sunscreen from the bathroom, and before long we're driving through Manhattan toward the harbor.

"So what are we doing?" he asks, watching me drive his car. I offered to drive my own, but he insisted on the Porsche, and I wasn't about to argue.

I fucking love this car.

"It's a surprise," I say primly. "I *can* keep a secret when I need to."

"Well, I'm excited."

I glance over at him and have to catch my breath. God, this man does to a black T-shirt and sunglasses is just ridiculous.

"Has anyone ever told you that you're too good-looking?"

He snorts. "I don't think so."

"Well, it's true. I mean, you just rolled out of bed, threw on a simple outfit, and you look like *that*."

"And how do I look?"

"Like sex on a stick."

He laughs, a full-on belly laugh, and kisses my hand. "Ah, Sienna, you're good for my ego."

"Hey, I only speak the truth. It's a bit intimidating."

"You're stunning," he replies without pause. "You have nothing to be intimidated by."

I pull into the parking lot of the Jet Ski place and cut the engine. "We're here. We're going to do some adrenaline junkie stuff today, just for you."

He's quiet for a second, and I look up at him.

"Are you okay?"

"This is pretty incredible," he says quietly, then leans over the center console to kiss the ever-loving fuck out of me. "Thank you."

"You're welcome. Now come on, we don't want to be late."

We listen to some instructions and are fitted with life preservers, and I pray with all my might that I *don't* fall into that disgusting New York City water.

But I don't say anything.

Before long, I'm slathered in sunscreen, we have our swimsuits on—thank God it's hot today—and we're ready to go.

"You can hold on to me," Quinn says with a smile, but I shake my head.

"No way, I'm getting my own."

"Is that so?"

"Absolutely. I can drive this."

His smile grows, and he offers me his fist to bump.

"Good girl, let's go."

And for the next hour, we play on the water, zooming back and forth and around each other, jumping off the wakes and having a blast.

"We have about thirty minutes left," I inform him. We only have the skis for two hours.

"Let's race out to the buoy," he suggests, pointing about a mile out into the water.

"Ready set go," I say fast and take off, laughing like a loon as I gun it, aimed for the buoy. But not thirty seconds later, Quinn passes me, smiling and waving at me. He beats me with enough time to stop and just watch me as I approach.

"You cheated, and I still won," he says.

"I know. See? Cheaters never prosper." I'm laughing as I take my hair down and give it a shake before sweeping it up again, catching all the strands that have shaken loose in the wind. I'm parked a few feet from Quinn, and he reaches over to pull me next to him, cups my cheek, and kisses me soundly.

"Don't make me fall in this dirty water," I say before I go in for kiss number two. When I pull back, we're both breathing hard. I glance over at the Statue of Liberty and smile. "You know, I've never been."

"You grew up here and have never been?" he asks, surprised.

"Nope. Let's go."

"I'll race you back."

"So we're going to climb?" I ask, staring up at the tall statue. We haven't gone inside yet.

"Of course," Quinn says. "You want the full experience, don't you?"

"Sure." I shrug as we go inside and walk through the museum

in the base of the statue. "This is really interesting. I can't believe I've never done this before."

"I can't either," he says. "We came with our school."

I shrug a shoulder and look at a ledger of incoming immigrants from 1912. "The fascinating thing is, most of this stuff is from the time of the case we're working now."

He glances at me, then back at the ledger and the other artifacts around us.

"You're right."

"It's been like working in a time capsule. You know, I think it was Matt who suggested that rather than throw away the stuff that doesn't matter, like grocery receipts and such, that I should donate them to a museum. I wonder if that's not such a bad idea."

"I think it's a great idea." Quinn wraps his arm around my shoulders and kisses my temple. "It's something you should definitely talk to your family about."

I nod as we make our way to the steps that lead to the statue's crown.

"Three hundred seventy-seven steps," I read. "It says that only people in good physical condition should attempt this, so you go ahead."

He laughs and takes my hand. "You're in great condition. You've got this."

I glance around. "Are you talking to me?"

"Yes, sweetheart, I'm talking to you. Now get your gorgeous ass in gear."

I want to grumble. I want to whine. But I don't. I climb the damn stairs, having to stop about every thirty steps to catch my breath.

Of course, Quinn isn't even breathing hard.

"It's hard to like people like you," I say when I don't feel like my lungs are on fire anymore. "This isn't even hard for you."

"I work out," he reminds me. "But we can go at your pace, it doesn't bother me at all. I just love being with you."

And just like that, he makes all this torture worth it. We continue to climb, stopping here and there for me, and all I can think is, *My ass is going to be in great shape by the time we get to the top.* The steps are quite narrow, and it's good that I'm not claustrophobic.

I *know* Quinn is staring at my rear, which is going to be not only in great shape, but very sore tomorrow.

But once we're at the top, I forget all about the torture of getting here. The view is incredible.

"It's smaller than I expected," I say.

"That's what *she* said," Quinn quips, making me laugh.

"No, they'd never say that about you, my love."

He doesn't reply, just cocks a brow at me as we look out at Manhattan and the harbor below.

"I think I can see your condo from here," I say, squinting into the distance.

"I think we can see Toronto from here," he says with a laugh. "I never realized it was this high."

"Pretty high," I murmur. I don't love heights. I'm not deathly afraid of them, but I don't love them. "I thought you'd been here before."

"I've never been to the top," he says and links his fingers through mine, then leans in to give me a hell of a kiss.

Damn, the man's good with his lips.

"Thank you for today. It's the best time I've had in a very long time." His mouth is near my ear, whispering the sweet words.

"You're welcome. I had a great time too."

"I hate to do this to you, folks, but I need you to move along so more people can come up," the woman in uniform says to us. We nod and take another look around.

"You know," I say to Quinn and brush my fingers through the hair at his temple. "I think you have a couple of gray hairs."

He stares down at me in surprise. "Well, ladies and gentlemen, she's about to go over the side."

He reaches for me, and I rush away, laughing.

"That's not funny!"

"Neither is the gray hair comment," he replies as I make a beeline for the stairs. "So, over the side or I spank you, which do you want?"

I immediately turn my butt to him. "It looks fabulous after all those stairs, so go ahead."

He swats me firmly, but not enough to sting, then pulls me in for a tight hug.

"Never a dull moment with you, sweetheart."

"And you love that about me."

"I absolutely do."

"Baby."

I push my face into the pillow, hoping the voice goes away.

"Baby, I need you to wake up," Quinn croons. I open my eyes, surprised to see that it's dark outside.

"Jesus, how long did I sleep?"

"Three hours," he says with a soft smile and pushes my hair off my cheek. "You needed a nap after our busy day out."

"I feel like a wimp." I sit up and stretch, yawn and then scoot into his lap. "This is nice."

"Unfortunately, I have to go."

"What?" I frown up at him. "Where are you going?"

"Finn called, and he needs me at the office for a little while. It won't take too long. Do you want to go with me, or stay here?"

"I should get some work done there," I reply and bite my lip. "But honestly, I think I'll stay here and paint."

"I like that plan," he says and kisses my forehead. "A day off has been good for you."

"Mm."

He sets me on the bed and stands to put his wallet in his pocket.

"Want me to pick up dinner on my way back?"

"I'll make something," I reply. "I'm feeling domestic today."

I follow him out into the kitchen, distract us both with another toe-curling kiss, and then he's gone, and I'm alone in his big, quiet condo.

I love this space. It's inviting and comfortable, and the kitchen is my favorite part.

It's just every chef's wet dream.

I decide on tacos for dinner, which is easy enough, and then remember that there's a box of brownie mix in the pantry.

"Brownies for dessert," I murmur. "Yes, please."

I quickly mix the batter and get it in the oven, set the alarm on my phone for the baking time, and then walk into my studio. I turn on some music, the Maroon 5 station on Pandora, and glance around the space.

Quinn outdid himself in here. I've already spent a few hours here, and it's still new. I'm like a kid with new toys, and I'm addicted.

I mix my paints, loving the texture of them, and how easy they are to work with. I don't usually splurge on such expensive materials, but I think I'll have to start setting aside more money for them. Now that I've used them, there's just no going back to the cheaper variety.

Quinn has spoiled me since I started to work at his office. He's incredibly thoughtful. He has waters, coffees, and snacks sent into the conference room every day. He has enough sent for all of us, but I know that's just so it doesn't look like he's showing favoritism toward me.

He takes care of me, and the best part is, I don't *need* him to. It's not because he has to save me from something.

It's because he loves me.

I don't think I expected love to feel like this. That I'd ever want someone to take care of me because I've always been so fiercely independent. I can do for myself.

I don't *need* a man.

But that's not what this is, and it's surprising.

I love that he cares and respects my needs enough to want to fulfill them, just like I did today for him with our day out.

It's not something I would normally do, but I had a good time. I had a *great* time because Quinn smiled all day, and that was the best part.

I've quickly painted New York Harbor, and the Statue of Liberty in watercolors. I can't help but add two figures in the water, skimming over the surface.

I glance at the timer on my phone. I have just enough time to clean up before the brownies are due to come out of the oven.

Even cleaning up isn't a chore in this space. The overhead light is bright, and doesn't cast weird shadows over the room. It's perfect for painting.

Once my studio is clean, I set the finished canvas on the floor, leaning against the wall so it can dry while I start something new, and walk out to the kitchen just as the timer dings.

"That smells amazing."

I whirl at the sound of Quinn's voice and cover my heart with my hand.

"I didn't hear you come in."

"I'm sorry." He sweeps me up in a hug and kisses me tenderly.

"I was productive while you were gone."

He cocks a brow as I pull the brownies out of the oven.

"You did more than brownies?"

"They bake for an hour, so I had plenty of time to work on a little something. I'll show you." I lead him to the studio and point to the painting.

"You did this in an *hour*?"

"Yeah, I wanted it to look a little abstract, almost messy. Chaotic."

"It's beautiful," he says. "And I love that we're in it."

"I thought that was a fun addition. Come on, you can chat with me while I cook."

"We're not having brownies for dinner?"

I laugh as I pull out a cutting board and the vegetables for the tacos. "I'd planned on my famous tacos."

"It's a good thing I got so much exercise today," he says, patting his flat stomach. "Bring on the food."

"I'm hungry too. This won't take long. Was everything okay at work?"

"Yeah, Finn has a difficult client, and he needed someone to bounce some things off of. We work better in person."

"I get it." I give the browning meat a stir. "Did he get it figured out?"

"I think so."

"Good."

"Sienna."

"Yeah?" I turn to look at him. He's sitting at the island, his handsome face serious. "What is it?"

"Come here."

I walk around the island, thinking he wants to hug me, but he boosts me onto the island and hugs me around the middle, his head pressed to my breasts.

"Thank you again for today."

"You're welcome." I kiss his head, breathing in the scent of him. "I'm glad you enjoyed it."

"I don't think anyone has ever done something like that for me before."

I frown, brushing my fingers through his soft hair. "Not even one girlfriend before me took you somewhere adventurous?"

He nuzzles my breasts playfully. "Most of the adventures of my past with women have been in the bedroom." He looks up at me with serious eyes. "Anything more was delving into personal territory that I wasn't willing to share."

"Why me?"

He sighs, still watching me in that sober way that makes my heart feel tender. "The only way I can describe it is, I saw you for the first time, and I knew my life would never be the same. You are seated squarely in the heart of my being, Sienna."

"What a lovely thing to say," I murmur.

"I want to have my way with you, right here in my kitchen."

I grin and kiss him again, then he reaches his lips up to mine, and I nuzzle his nose.

"The meat will burn, so you'll have to wait for kitchen sex until after dinner."

"I could eat my brownie off *you*," he says with a sly smile. "That would make it taste even better."

"Not with ice cream." I bite his lower lip. "That would be too cold."

His hand glides up my inner thigh, to the hem of my cutoffs, and I shiver.

"You like that?" he asks.

"No time for this," I remind him, but I'm not pushing him away. I'm not stupid, after all.

"I'm going to eat your tacos," he says, and I can't help but laugh.

"Is that a euphemism for my pussy?"

"Fuck yes it is."

Chapter Sixteen

~Sienna~

I smell warm brownies and coffee.

Am I still dreaming? Because if I am, I don't want to wake up.

I open one eye into a curious slit, and sure enough, there's Quinn wearing only pajama bottoms, holding a tray of brownies and coffee.

"Good, you're awake," he says. He's *such* a morning person. Happy and ready to go first thing, and it takes me a good hour to wake up fully.

However, I will admit that he's not annoying with his morning personness, and for that, I'm grateful.

"You're feeding me brownies in bed," I murmur as I pull myself up, sitting against his gray tufted headboard.

"It's Sunday," he replies, as if that explains everything, and sets the tray in the middle of the bed, then climbs on to join me. Before passing me my mug, he leans over to kiss me. "Good morning."

"Mm, good morning." I gratefully accept the cup of caffeine and take a sip, sighing as it hits my bloodstream. "I could get used to Sundays like this."

"I hope so," he replies and opens the newspaper that was also on the tray.

"You read a *real* newspaper," I comment in surprise.

"I stare at screens enough all day long, I'd rather read the Sunday paper the old-fashioned way."

I take a bite of chocolate goodness and watch him thoughtfully. "I like you."

"That's good, since I've fallen head over heels for you." He drags his palm up and down my naked thigh. This man is constantly touching me.

It's awesome.

"What I'm saying is, not only do I love you, but I *like* you. Quite a lot."

"Good." He kisses my shoulder, takes a bite of my brownie, and goes back to reading his paper. "I figured it would be okay if we got a bit of a late start today."

"Yeah. I have to tell you, I'm ready to get back to my weekends off. I know this is normal for you, that you're used to the long hours in the office, but I'm not. I didn't sign up for it on purpose because I knew that it wasn't for me, even though I'm passionate about the law.

"So kudos to you for being so dedicated to your job that you can put in eighty hours a week."

"It is a lot," he says thoughtfully, sipping his coffee. He takes it black, which makes my lips pucker. "I admit that since I've been with you, I understand why Finn's backed off a bit so he can dedicate more time to London."

"You didn't understand it before?"

"I thought I did," he admits. "But I've never been in love before, so I didn't identify with the need to want to be with someone all the time. Work has been my love and my mistress for a long time, Sienna. I enjoy it, and I do well at it."

"I know, and I love that about you. I'm not being snarky when I say that I admire how much dedication you can give to it."

"I get it," he replies with a nod. "And I'll always have the drive to be an excellent attorney. It's part of who I am. So while I am beginning to understand that you are content with normal working hours so you can dedicate more time to things that drive you, like painting and cooking, I'm relieved that you understand why I push myself so hard at my career."

I open my mouth to speak, but he holds his finger against my lips.

"Let me finish. I want you to know that I do give a lot of myself to my work, but I have you now, and I'm just as dedicated to making this work and giving us the time and attention that we need and deserve. So over the coming months, I'll be working toward backing off on some of my hours at the office.

Specifically, weekends. Spending days off with you is important and fun, and I want more of them."

"I'm glad." I grin and drag my hand down his stubbly cheek, enjoying the way the whiskers feel against my palm. "Thanks for that. And for everything, really."

"Sienna, you deserve *everything*. I want you to be honest and open with me if you're unhappy or discontent so we can work on fixing something before it's irreparably broken."

"Same, Quinn."

He kisses my wrist, and then he goes back to his paper, and I nibble on my breakfast, sip my coffee, and scroll through Instagram. It's the only social media app that I have, mostly because I enjoy the photos my friends and family post of their loved ones and vacations. It's not typically politically driven, and I like that too.

I also follow some of my favorite artists on the 'gram, although I haven't posted my own artwork there.

Once I've caught up online and finished my coffee, I get out of bed and get ready to spend another long day at the office.

No, I'm not built for this much deskwork. I'll be so glad when the case is over.

"I THINK YOU'RE going to want to see this," Quinn says much later at the office. We've been here for *hours* and haven't found a damn thing.

"Please tell me it's the fourth receipt."

"No, sorry, but it's pretty incredible."

He passes me an old, yellow letter in an envelope.

November 14, 1910

My dearest Muriel,

I can't believe that today is our wedding day. After waiting for months, it's finally here. It's like a dream, my sweetheart, that very soon you'll be my wife.

You are the object of my desire, loving you is the only reason that I exist in this world. I will spend the rest of my life searching for what brings a smile to your lips, for you are more precious than I can tell you.

Life is fleeting, of this I am sure, especially since losing my papa this year, and I'm grateful that I get to spend the rest of my days with you by my side. I'm proud to stand as your husband, your friend, your lover. From now until my last breath, I do.

Yours always,
Lawrence

I wipe the tears from my cheeks and read through it again.

"It seems Great-Grandpa Lawrence was a romantic," I say as I sniff and Quinn passes me another handkerchief. "Where do you pull these out of? Thin air?"

"*My* father taught me that a man should always keep a hand-kerchief on him."

"Well, he raised you right."

I dab at my eyes and fold the letter back into its envelope. "I'll have to take this with us to my parents' house so they can read it."

"I'm sure they'd like that," he says before kissing my forehead and diving back into his box.

This project has been stressful, time-consuming, and tedious. But I've found so many wonderful family treasures that other-wise might have been lost forever.

"You know what's really sad?"

"What's that?"

"From what I've been told, Muriel died giving birth to their second child, about six years after they were married."

"So not long after he needed the loan from Reginald."

I nod. "Man, poor Lawrence had a rough few years."

"Did he remarry?"

"I found a marriage certificate a few days ago for Lawrence and a woman named Rose. So, I'm assuming yes." I reach for the folder and find the certificate. "He married her in 1920. She was twenty-three."

"How old was he?"

"Thirty-five."

"I wonder if they had more children?"

"I don't know. I realize that I know way too little about my family any older than my grandparents' age."

"Well, it makes sense. They've all been dead since before you were born, so it's not like you could ask questions."

"True. And I never really thought about it much until I started this." I check my watch, surprised by the time. "I guess we should wrap it up for the day and head over to my parents' house."

"Do you get together for dinners often?"

"About once a month. It's a way for my mom to check in with us."

"Am I about to get drilled?"

"Oh yeah. Put your attorney hat on, Counselor."

"It's always on, sweetheart."

"Here, Lou, you wash and peel the potatoes," Mom says as she pulls a bag of potatoes out of her pantry.

"Why do I have to wash them if I'm going to peel them?" Louise asks.

"Because I said so," Mom replies, but she softens the retort with a kiss to Lou's cheek. "Now that the boys are out in the garage, and out of listening range, tell me about Quinn, Sienna."

"He's an attorney," I reply, concentrating on chopping carrots.

"Yes, that I know," Mom says dryly. "I want to know all the other things. And let me just say right now, that man is *handsome*. I didn't really get a good look at him at the will reading because we were all surprised and distraught, but now that I have, well, he's one good-looking man."

"Mom."

"If I was thirty years younger, I might give you a run for your money."

"Mom!" Louise and I exclaim at the same time.

"What? I'm sixty-five, not blind."

"Thirty years ago, you were married to Dad," I remind her, but she just waves me off.

"What does he do for fun?"

"All the adrenaline junkie things he can find. Race car driving, hiking, zip-lining, you name it."

"Skydiving?" Louise asks.

"I hope not. I might have to veto that one. It's too dangerous."

"Do you have vetoing power?" Mom asks.

"Well, we've dropped the *love* word a few times, so I think that gives me vetoing power."

"*What?*" Louise screeches and pulls me in for a hug. "You didn't tell me!"

"Well, we've been busy, and what am I supposed to do? Put you two on speakerphone and say *hey, just wanted to let you know that Quinn and I are throwing the* love *word around*?"

"Yes," they say in unison, making me giggle.

"Well, it's no surprise to me," Lou says as she returns to the potatoes. "He called me last week and asked me for help with designing a studio for you in his condo."

"I've clearly been out of the loop," Mom complains, and I quickly fill her in on staying with Quinn, and the new studio. "Oh, I like him a lot."

"It was very sweet. And Lou must have been the reason he bought all the expensive supplies."

"What? You should have those things. Your work is amazing, and it can only be better with the good stuff."

"I do fine with what I've been using," I remind her, but then decide not to argue because the more expensive paints *are* better.

"Well, I'm happy for you," Mom says as she slips the veggies in the oven, along with the pork loin that went in a few hours ago. "I think it's just fantastic that you're working together to get the case resolved, and that you've fallen in love at the same time. It's something out of a movie."

"A really sexy movie," Louise agrees, and we all dissolve into laughter as the guys come in from the garage.

"I'm telling you, Louis," Uncle Patrick says, "that Corvette will never run."

"You say that about every car I buy, and I always get it running," Dad reminds him. Quinn is smiling as he comes into the kitchen and leans in to kiss my cheek.

"I like your dad," he whispers, and I immediately feel more at ease. That means that Dad and Uncle Patrick were welcoming and kind. Not that I thought they'd challenge Quinn to a duel or anything, but I was expecting some kind of lecture because they love me.

I'm glad it's going well.

"Dinner will be ready in about thirty minutes," Mom announces. "And I haven't had a chance to chat with Quinn. Would you like to join me out in the garden?"

"I'd be delighted," Quinn says, winks at me, and then follows my mom outside.

"He's charming everyone," Lou says once they're gone and Dad and Patrick are in the living room.

"He's a charming guy."

"And he's nice."

"Yeah."

"And hot."

"Duh."

"You gonna marry him?"

"He hasn't asked me." I turn to her now and frown. "Just because I'm having a romance doesn't mean we're going to get married next week."

"You could," she says. "I'm not saying you have to, but I'd keep this one."

"Did you hear from London about her engagement party?"

Louise grins and pulls us each a bottle of water out of the fridge. "Changing the subject. Okay, I'll allow it. Yes, we've spoken several times, and we already have a game plan in action. Thanks for the contact, by the way. This is a big one."

"I know." I smile smugly and take a sip of my water. "I've been telling you for a long time that you should be an event planner."

"Yeah, but starting a business isn't cheap."

"You just inherited a whole bunch of money," I say, raising an eyebrow. "That might be something good to invest in. Yourself."

She bites her lip, thinking about it. "And if I fail, I lose it all."

"If you walk into it thinking that you're going to fail, you already have." I link my arm through hers. "You're talented, good with people, and you're definitely the kind of woman who would rather work for herself than for anyone else."

"Got me there."

"Do it. I'll help. I can draw up contracts for clients, and I can help with a lot of things."

"You'd do that?"

"Of course."

She grins, then shimmies in a circle. "Oh my God, I think I'm going to do it!"

"Do what?" Mom asks as she and Quinn walk through the back door. Quinn is smiling, but in a different way from when he came in with my dad.

He looks . . . *calmer.*

"Open an event planning business," Louise says. "I'm ready to do it, and Sienna just talked me into it."

"Well, that's fantastic," Mom replies. "Congratulations, darling. Now, let's get dinner on the table."

"THAT WAS DELICIOUS," Quinn says when we're all sitting on the patio together for dessert. "Now I know where Sienna gets her amazing cooking skills."

"I liked to cook with Mom when I was a kid," I agree with a nod and take another bite of my strawberry cake.

"Thank you, Quinn," Mom says with a wink. It's beautiful outside, not too hot the way it has been the past few days, so we're taking advantage of the comfortable early evening.

"I'm going to go in and get started on cleaning up," Dad says. Uncle Patrick immediately stands as well.

"I'll help," he says.

"I can help too," Quinn offers, but Dad shoos him back into his seat.

"No need, Quinn. This time you're a guest, but next time you can help clean up." He winks and disappears into the house with Uncle Patrick. Louise fills our glasses with another round of wine.

"This is always how it goes," I offer in explanation. "The girls cook and the guys clean."

"Well, I'm perfectly fine with helping clean," Quinn says, but Mom waves him off.

"Not this time. Like Louis said, you can help next time."

"Tell us about some of the fun things you've found in those boxes," my sister requests. "There must be some interesting things in there."

"There have been," I agree. "In fact, I found a love letter from Great-Grandpa Lawrence to his first wife, Muriel, today. Actually, Quinn found it. It's really beautiful. I brought it for you all to read."

"That was such a sad story," Mom says with a sigh.

"I don't remember the whole story," I admit.

"Muriel died in childbirth about five or six years after they married."

"I knew that part. Is there more to the story?"

"From what we were told, she was a sweet woman. Quiet, but confident, and she didn't take any shit from anyone. In fact, I've seen photos of her, and you look a lot like her, Sienna."

"So she was a stunning woman," Quinn says with a wink.

"She was quite pretty. And I just realized, you're wearing your hair down today. That's unusual."

"I recently started something new." I link my fingers through Quinn's, and Mom keeps telling the story.

"Well, I love it. Anyway, poor Muriel had her second baby breech and ended up bleeding to death. Of course, medical advances are such now that she would have lived."

"That is sad."

"The story goes that Lawrence was quite distraught and didn't know quite what to do. Muriel took care of the family, and he worked, as it was with most families at that time. So he hired Muriel's sister, Rose, to come live with him and the children, to be a nanny of sorts to help him."

"Oh, my," I whisper, already knowing where this is going.

"Well, he ended up marrying Rose," Mom says.

"Nanny affairs even back then," Lou says, shaking her head.

"I found their marriage certificate. Did they have more kids?"

"No, she was never able to get pregnant. She committed suicide ten years after they married."

"Good God, this is horrible." I stare at Mom in horror. "What happened to Lawrence?"

"I actually met him," she replies. "When your father and I were dating, he was still alive. He passed just before we married."

"Did he ever get married again?"

"I don't think so."

"Well, that's depressing," Lou says, emptying the last of the wine in her glass. "We need more alcohol and happy stories."

"There's more wine inside," Mom says, but before she can stand, Quinn does.

"I'll go get it."

"Thank you, dear."

The door closes behind him and Mom smiles at me. "He's wonderful, Sienna."

"I think so."

"If you get married, I want to help plan it," Lou says. "I won't even charge you."

"You're too kind." My voice is as dry as the desert, but I can't help but laugh at her. "And you'd be hired, but let's not get ahead of ourselves. He hasn't asked. It's only been a few weeks."

"I just have a very good feeling about this," Mom says with a smug smile.

"I wonder what's taking him so long." I frown and stand. "I'm just going to check on him."

I walk through the back door and hear voices in the kitchen. When I walk around the corner, it's just Patrick and Quinn in the room, Patrick's back is to me, and Quinn's face is flat-out pissed.

"Fuck off," Quinn growls at Uncle Patrick, and then he sees me standing in the doorway.

I'm stunned. What in the world could Uncle Patrick have said to warrant that response?

"What the hell?"

Chapter Seventeen

~Quinn~

I'm enjoying all of them. Louis is fascinating to talk cars with, which gives us quite a lot in common, and the whole family has been inviting and gracious.

Patrick hasn't said much, but I'm fine with that. I already want to deck the asshole.

I walk into the house, shut the door behind me, and walk into the kitchen, looking for another bottle of wine. I'm surprised that Patrick is in the kitchen alone.

"The girls want more wine," I say, spying a bottle on the countertop. I reach for it, and turn to leave, but Patrick is standing in my way of the door.

"I've looked into you," he begins and crosses his arms over his chest. "I know that you're a good attorney."

"Okay." I tilt my head, interested to see where this is going.

"So color me surprised when I discovered that you and Sienna are working on the case together. I wouldn't think you'd need to fuck her to win this case. Or is that your plan? It'll be easier to comfort her when she loses?"

"Fuck off," I reply, my hand already fisted and ready to land in his face when I glance up and see Sienna standing in the doorway, her eyes wide with confusion.

"What the hell?" She props her hands on her hips, glaring at me. "Why would you speak that way to my uncle?"

"You must not have heard the part where he basically called you a whore," I reply, my eyes returning to Patrick's. But he shakes his head and turns to Sienna, his face transforming into a soft smile.

"I did no such thing," he says, his voice smoothing immediately. "You know I wouldn't say something like that. I've already voiced my concerns to you, Sienna, about working so closely with the opposing counsel. I don't think it's appropriate."

"I've already told you that it's none of your business," she says, surprising me. "We aren't doing anything wrong by working together to get to the bottom of a case that goes back a century. I don't appreciate you cornering Quinn in the kitchen and grilling him."

"I'm looking out for your best interests."

Bullshit. He just admitted to me that he intends for Sienna to lose the case.

"I think it's time to go," Sienna says. She turns and marches out the door and I'm close on her heels. "I'm sorry, everyone, but we have to go back to work."

"You work too hard, dear," Sienna's mom says, but we say our good-byes and are on our way back to my condo before Sienna will even speak to me.

"I didn't like hearing you speak that way to my uncle."

And I don't like that your uncle is trying to fuck you over.

"I can't believe you're close to that man," I reply, my hands tightening almost painfully on the steering wheel. "You weren't there to hear what he said before you came in."

"He's not been himself lately," she insists. "I told you that before. I don't know what's going on with him. Maybe he's grieving, maybe he's worried about the case."

Yeah, worried that you'll find that last payment and he'll be screwed.

"I don't buy it, Sienna. You just don't say shit like that about your niece. I would cut off my own tongue before I said something like that about Gabby."

"Maybe he has something going on medically," she argues. "We don't know. But I *do* know that I've been close to him my whole life and I walked in on my boyfriend telling him to fuck off."

"Damn right I did, and I'm not apologizing for standing up for the woman I love, Sienna. He's lucky I didn't deck him. I'd like to go back and do exactly that."

"I can't believe this," she grumbles. "He may be too opinionated about how we're handling the case, I don't disagree with you there. But he also comes from another era, where he probably wouldn't have worked with opposing counsel."

"Or a woman," I mutter without being able to hold it in.

"He encouraged me to go to law school," she says. "Seriously, Quinn, I think you're overreacting."

And I can't fucking explain to her that I'm not. It's the most frustrating situation I've ever been in.

"I told you before that I don't trust him, and he hasn't changed my opinion."

"Well, I trust him," she says, and my hands tighten on the wheel again. "There are three men in this world that I trust the most, and it's you, my dad, and Uncle Patrick."

Slash to the heart.

"So, even though you don't trust him, I need you to trust me."

"I do trust you." I peel my hand off the wheel and take her hand in mine, pulling it to my lips. "Implicitly."

"That's all that matters."

I NEED TO figure out a way to tell her that Patrick is a lying douchebag and not break the law. Because keeping it from her is killing me.

I'm in my office the next morning, and rather than the work I'm supposed to be doing, I'm staring at a blank piece of paper, trying to think of ways to fill Sienna in.

"I could ask Finn or Carter to tell her," I mumble, but then immediately scratch that off the list. Technically, Bruce is their client, too, since he hired the firm, not just me.

Damn it.

I could take my notes home from that meeting with Bruce and leave them on the kitchen counter for her to accidentally see.

The only problem with that is, she won't read them. I know her, and she's too principled to sneak a look at notes that don't belong to her.

God, I love her.

I could send her an anonymous letter. I sit back in my chair, thinking it over. She checks her mail a couple times a week, so that could work. It might be the only way to do it and not have it come back on me.

There's a knock at my door and Sienna walks in with a smile on her face. She locks the door behind her.

"I asked Kami if you were busy and she said no."

"She was right," I reply, watching as she walks around my desk and leans against it next to me. I wrap my arm around her slim waist and scoop her into my lap. "What's up, sweetheart?"

"You know, you look really sexy behind this desk."

"Is that right?"

"I've thought so since the first time I saw this office. It's big and masculine, and it fits you perfectly."

"I'm glad that you approve of my office."

She's playing with the knot of my tie, touching my neck and chin, and fucking hell, I want her.

Here.

Now.

"Sienna, I'm going to fuck you on my desk."

She grins, her blue eyes on fire with lust. "Oh, I hope so."

In one fluid motion, I boost her onto the desk and hike her skirt up around her hips.

"We're going to wrinkle your briefs," she says with a laugh.

"I'm not wearing briefs."

"I meant your legal briefs, ace."

"I know what you meant." I bite the side of her neck and my cock strains against my pants at her soft moan. "And I don't give a shit about anything but you right now."

"Every girl loves to hear that," she whispers. Her fingers are fisted in my hair and my hand is gliding up her thigh to her core.

"Jesus, you're wet, honey."

"I've wanted this for a *long* time." She scoots her ass closer to the edge of the desk and reaches for my pants, unfastens them, and sets my heavy cock free. "It's something of a fantasy."

"You definitely should have said something earlier." I reach for my wallet, thankful that I tucked a condom in there, and hurry to fill her, to feel her stiffen around me. "You fit me like a goddamn glove."

"So good," she breathes. "God, Quinn."

My mouth is on hers as I push inside, absorbing her groans of pleasure. What started as frenzied and hurried quickly turns soft and intimate.

I drag the backs of my knuckles down her cheek and kiss her nose, her eyes.

"I'm in the deep end of this with you," I whisper. "You're

mine, Sienna. This." I press in balls deep and pin her hands to the desk. She's panting, watching me with wide blue eyes. "Is mine. And this." I kiss her chest, over her heart. "This is mine."

"All yours," she confirms. "And you're mine back."

I grin and kiss her, moving my hips in a steady rhythm that will send us both over the edge. She clamps her legs around my hips and tilts her pelvis, taking more of me and making my eyes cross.

"Fuck yes," I mutter, burying my face against her neck as I come apart. I don't bother to muffle her moans as she follows me over. I don't care who hears us.

She's mine.

I want to shout it from the rooftops.

I kiss her softly and help her into a sitting position before I walk into my private bath to flush the condom and tuck myself away. When I walk back out, she's fixing her lipstick and looks as perfect as she did when she first walked in here.

"We didn't wrinkle your briefs too badly," she says with a smug smile. "I actually came in here to let you know that I'm leaving for the afternoon. I have to go to my parents' house."

"What's up?"

"I forgot my phone there yesterday. I think I'll see if my mom wants to go to lunch."

"Okay, I'll see you tonight?"

"Of course. I'll text you when I'm on my way back. I guess it's good that we drove separately today."

She winks and saunters out of my office. Damn, I love her ass.

We drove separately because I needed a couple of hours at the gym before work to try to burn off some of the aggression and anger I'm carrying about this case.

I'm an attorney. Keeping secrets isn't new to me.

Keeping them from the woman I'm madly in love with? That's a whole different story, and I'm not comfortable with it.

The anonymous letter is the way to go.

But before I can start to type it up, my phone rings.

"This is Cavanaugh."

"It's Bruce. This isn't an easy phone call to make."

I frown and lean back in my chair. "What's up?"

"I just got a call from Patrick Hendricks. He told me that he has the proof that the money was repaid in the loan for the property, and for one million dollars, he'd be happy to make it go away."

I hit mute on the phone so I can say, "Motherfucker," then unmute. "What do you want me to do?"

Bruce sighs. "I told both you and Sienna that I'm not a dick, I'm a businessman. I wasn't lying. I'm a lot of things, but I don't do shady shit like this, especially when I have no skin in the game. It's not property that I paid for, and I don't have plans for it yet."

Holy shit, Bruce is going to do the right thing.

"I'm going to drop the case, Quinn. And I think it's time for Sienna to know what's going on."

Thank fuck.

"I'm glad you've made this decision. I think it's the right one. I'll get the paperwork going."

"What's going to happen to Patrick Hendricks?"

"Well, he's committed fraud, and bribery, so the city could press charges, but that will be up to them. I'll keep you posted, but in the meantime, do you have anything in writing?"

"Just the note from Patrick that came with the letter. He called today, and I didn't record it."

"That's fine," I say. "I think the important thing is that you're dropping the case. I'll get that in motion right away."

I end the call and drag my hand down my face. I'm relieved that I don't have to keep lying to Sienna and worried about how she's going to take the news.

She doesn't have her phone on her, but I call it anyway.

When it goes to voice mail, I leave a message. "Hey, it's me. I need you to call me right away. Right away, Sienna."

Then I send a text for good measure.

Call me as soon as you get your phone. It's urgent.

Chapter Eighteen

~Sienna~

I'm looking forward to lunch with my mom. I don't know for sure that she's home since I can't call her, but I hope she is. I was reminded yesterday that I don't see my family often enough, especially lately.

But with our final court date being a week from today, things should go back to normal soon where my schedule is concerned, and I can look in on my parents more often.

I park in the driveway, surprised to see my uncle Patrick's car also parked out front. I never knock on my parents' door. I tried once when I came home from college, and my mom lectured me on how this is still my house, and I don't ever have to knock when I visit.

So I walk through the door, but before I can peek into the living room, I overhear my name, stopping me in my tracks.

"I don't think Sienna knows," Uncle Patrick says. "Bruce

mentioned to me that Quinn does, but I guess hopping in bed with her doesn't necessarily mean that he tells her *everything*."

"That's what we were worried about," Dad replies and every hair on my body stands on end. "So Quinn is a good lawyer."

"As is your daughter," Uncle Patrick responds. "Better than we thought."

"It doesn't matter *how* good she is," Dad says, "if she doesn't have the proof of the last payment."

"What were the odds that I'd find that journal in the boxes I took from Dad's?" Uncle Patrick says, a huge smile in his voice. I can't help but peek around the wall, to see them sitting, smiling and chatting as if they're talking about a great golf game, rather than the fact that they're trying to screw over our family.

I'm stunned. Am I hearing what I think I'm hearing?

"What did Bruce say when you told him you could make the proof go away?" Dad asks.

"He said he'd have to think about it, but it's a no-brainer. He pays us the million, I burn the journal and the letter, and he owns the property. It's worth far more than one million dollars."

"Which is why I'm pissed that Dad left it to the city," Dad replies. His voice is hard now. "He gave too much of the money to the girls and the fucking *church*, and all we get is his house? Along with a paltry amount of cash? It's absurd."

I can't stand it anymore. Every fiber of my being is vibrating with fury. I walk around the wall, plant my hands on my hips, and glare at the surprised men, the men I've always trusted my whole life, who I just discovered *I don't even know.*

"I can't believe what I just heard."

"What did you hear, baby girl?" Dad asks.

"Every fucking thing you said in the past five minutes."

Both men go pale and I spy the journal on the table, with a letter peeking out of the top. I swipe it up and tuck it under my arm.

"Now, Sienna, you don't know all the details and reasons that we had to do this," Dad says as he stands, and I shake my head, backing away from him.

"Do you know how many reasons would be valid? Zero. You didn't own the property and you're mad about it? You're acting like spoiled children who didn't get your way. Which is exactly what you are."

"You don't know anything," Uncle Patrick begins, but I hold my hand up to stop him.

"I know that you offered to make this proof go away for a million dollars. I know that's fraud *and* bribery, which are both illegal. I know that you're fucking over your own family and community."

"You may be angry, but you'll watch your language," Dad says. I can only laugh humorlessly, staring at him as if he's crazy.

Because he just might be.

"I'm taking this." I hold the book up. "It's part of Grandpa's estate, and *that's* part of evidence in an ongoing case."

"You can't do that," Dad insists, but Uncle Patrick shakes his head.

"Yes, she can."

"Hello, everyone! Wow, there's quite a party going on." Mom walks in from the kitchen and stops short when she sees us all in our standoff. "What's happening?"

"Did you know?" I demand.

"Did I know what?"

"No," Dad says with a heavy sigh. "She didn't."

"Did I know what?" Mom asks again.

"That Dad and Uncle Patrick had the proof all along that Bruce House doesn't actually own the park, and that they were bribing him to make the proof of that go away?"

She stares at both men, her jaw dropped, and shakes her head.

"Louis, tell me this isn't true."

Dad just shakes his head and Uncle Patrick sits on the couch, his head in his hands.

"They've both committed real estate fraud, they've cost the city a *lot* of money, and we could throw bribery into the mix, which is all illegal and could put them away for a while."

"We wouldn't go to prison," Uncle Patrick says, but I shake my head.

"We don't know that." I turn to Mom, who's also gone pale, and take her hand in mine.

"You really didn't know?"

"How could you ask me that?" Her voice is hollow.

"I didn't think *they* could do something like this either."

I'm shaking. I want to hit them both, to rage at them and demand to know what in the hell they were *thinking*.

But I will never forget the tone of their voices just a few minutes ago when they thought they were about to get away with it. They were not the men I know and love.

"You need to turn yourselves in, before I do."

"Sienna Marie Hendricks," Dad says in shock. "You would *not* do that to your family."

"Oh, you clearly underestimate me." I shake my head and then laugh humorlessly. "Actually, that's exactly what you did. You didn't think that I'd win this case."

"We knew you wouldn't because *we* had the final proof that you'd never find," Uncle Patrick says, his voice as flat as a stranger's.

"I can't believe what I'm hearing," Mom says.

"Me neither," I reply, suddenly needing to get away. I leave the room, to the kitchen where my phone is sitting on the countertop, then hurry back to the living room. No one has moved.

"You have two hours to do the right thing," I say. "I'll be telling my boss exactly what's happened, and I'll petition the court to dismiss the case."

"Don't do this," Dad says. "Sienna, we'll give you a cut of the money."

Uncle Patrick's head whips up in surprise, staring at Dad as if he just offered to sacrifice a virgin.

"You just tried to bribe the city attorney?"

"I'm pleading with my daughter to not do something that you'll regret."

I shake my head, watching both of them in horror. "Who *are* you? Both of you? How could you do this?"

"I would hate for you to lose your job over your canoodling with Quinn," Patrick says in a pathetic attempt to scare me, and I immediately see red all over again.

"We're done here. You're not going to bribe me or *threaten* me into dropping this. Two hours."

And with that, I hurry out to my car and drive away, glancing at my phone.

Quinn knew.

Quinn knew.

And he didn't tell me.

That might be the biggest betrayal of all.

God, I feel like such a fool. My family was lying to me, and Quinn was lying to me.

I can't go back to Quinn's office, or his condo. I'm too angry. I'm too hurt.

First, I have to handle my case. That's the most important thing.

I drive directly to *my* office and hurry inside to Dave's office.

"Long time no see," he says when he looks up from his desk, an unlit cigar in his mouth. He frowns. "What's going on?"

I calmly explain everything that I heard at my parents' house, and when I'm done, the cigar is gone and he's shaking his head, pinching the bridge of his nose.

"Jesus, Si." He sighs deeply. "I'm sorry."

I clear my throat, unwilling to start crying now. "I'm going to petition the court to drop the case."

"Agreed."

"I'll write it up now. And I recommend that the city press charges."

"Are you sure?" He stands, walks around his desk, and leans against it, his arms crossed over his chest. "This is your family."

"I'm sure. They broke the law, and they wasted *hours and hours* of the city's time. At the least they should have to pay for that."

"I'll get that going," he says. His face is grim. "Sienna."

"No." I shake my head. "No, Dave, don't get mushy on me. I need to see this through and then I need a week off."

"Done." He gestures for me to leave his office. "Do what you need to do, but I'm here if you need anything."

I nod and hurry to my desk, and send my petition. Then, I take my things and drive home.

My home.

I feel numb now. The anger is still there, simmering just below the surface, but it's as if the past few hours have happened to someone else and I'm watching it from the outside.

Damn, how I wish that were true.

I pull into my driveway, scowling when I see Quinn in his car out front.

And just like that, the anger bubbles back to the surface.

He emerges out of his car at the same moment I do, and I ignore him. If I start talking, I'll rage at him, I'll hit him.

I'll say things that I can't ever take back.

"Sienna, I need to talk to you. I've been blowing up your phone, but you're not responding."

And I don't respond now as I unlock the door and walk into my house, Quinn right behind me.

"Baby, did you hear me?"

I set my bag in its place, then turn to him and prop my hands on my hips.

"How long?" I ask.

"How long what?"

"How long have you known that my father and uncle were the ones who got this whole fucking thing rolling?"

"Wait. Your father?" He looks honestly confused, and I wait for his answer. "Bruce told me it was Patrick who originally sent him the letter."

"When?"

His jaw clenches and the muscle in it tics in that way it does when he's irritated. "A while ago."

I nod, not believing my ears. "Get out of my house."

"Sienna—"

"No." I turn around and stomp into the kitchen, needing to put some space between us. "You *knew*, Quinn, that my family was not just wasting my time but making a goddamn fool of me."

"No, I didn't," he replies. "I had no idea that your father was involved, and I didn't know until after you left my office today that Patrick has the final proof you need."

"But you knew that Patrick was involved."

He shoves his hands in his pockets.

"I couldn't tell you."

"Bullshit."

"No, it's not bullshit. *I couldn't tell you.* It was attorney-client privilege, Sienna. You know as well as I do that if I'd said anything it would have been illegal."

"We were working as a *team*!" I yell.

"Bruce told me as a client. It's a fine fucking line, Sienna."

I shake my head and pull the pins out of my hair, needing to scratch my scalp, hoping to relieve the pounding headache I have.

"I need you to go," I say. "I'm done, and I need you to go."

He's still for a moment. "I never lied to you."

"You withheld important information."

"I tried to tell you that I didn't trust Patrick."

"That's weak, Quinn. I could tell you that I don't trust Carter, and what does that do, exactly? Does it make you love him less? No, you'd roll your eyes and pat me on the head and say *there's no reason not to trust Carter.*"

"I would ask you why you don't trust him."

"And if I'd done that, you still would have lied."

He shakes his head in frustration. "As soon as Bruce gave me the go-ahead I tried to tell you. I've been trying to reach you since you left today."

"How noble of you."

God, I feel sick to my stomach. I'm going to throw up. I'm going to cry for days. I need him to go away.

"I told you yesterday that there are three men in my life that I trust. Every one of them disappointed me today."

"Sienna—"

"Go." I shake my head and lean on the island. "I'm done, and I want you to go."

He walks to the door, but before he leaves, he turns back to me.

"This isn't done. *We* aren't done. But I'll go for now."

Just as the door closes behind him, my phone rings. It's Louise.

"Hello?" Tears are already forming in my eyes as I hear Quinn's car fire up outside and he speeds away.

"I just got off the phone with Mom. Sienna, what's going on?"

"I need you." It's a whisper. "I need you at my house."

"I'm already on the way. With wine, and a shitload of questions."

"Hurry." I hang up and collapse onto the island, my cheek on the cold quartz and hot tears streaming from my eyes.

Oh, my God, what just happened?

My whole world just fell apart in the span of two hours.

I thought I'd be punching something. Screaming and railing.

But I'm just lying on the cool countertop and silently crying because my brain just can't do anything else.

I'm still here ten minutes later when Louise comes rushing through the door, two bottles tucked under her arms and her face also streaked with tears.

"Talk to me," she says softly as she hurries to me and softly drags her fingers through my hair. "Mom's a mess and couldn't tell me much. Is it true?"

I nod and wipe my nose with the back of my hand.

"Dad and Patrick tried to screw the city out of the park. Uncle Patrick found the original letter, and the final letter that showed the loan had been paid in full, in a journal when he was going through Grandpa's things after he died, but before the will reading. I guess, given that Uncle Patrick drew up Grandpa's will, he knew that he and Dad wouldn't be splitting the whole estate, and they felt that they were being ripped off."

"Fuck," she whispers and sniffs.

"They tried to get a million dollars out of House to make the proof go away."

"Jesus, Si."

I pull myself up and stare at my older sister, who looks so much like me, and yet is so different from me.

"They lied to us."

We hold hands and make our way to my couch.

"Want to know the worst part?" I ask her.

"Jesus, it gets worse? Let me pour some wine first."

She passes me a box of tissues, takes some for herself, and quickly opens a bottle of wine, bringing it with two glasses back to the couch.

"Okay." She pours us each a glass and passes me mine. "Take a sip first, then go ahead."

I oblige and lick my lips. "Quinn knew."

Her eyes bulge, and her mouth forms an O shape. "What? He *knew?*"

"He didn't know all of it until today, but he knew that Patrick was the one to initiate it all."

"And he didn't tell you."

I shake my head and take another sip. "Nope. Because House told him, and it was attorney-client privilege."

She's blinking rapidly as she takes a huge gulp of her wine.

"Wow," she says at last. "I'm sorry."

"Me too."

"What's going to happen now?"

"Well, Dad and Patrick will be charged with real estate fraud and bribery. I don't know if they'll go to jail, or just be fined. They'll probably be fined."

"Jesus," she mutters.

"I'm worried about Mom." The tears start again, and I take another sip of wine. "She didn't know what they were doing."

"We're strong like her," Louise says. "But it's going to be rough for her. Maybe I should stay with her for a little while."

I nod and lean my head on Lou's shoulder. "I want to deck them both."

"Mom slapped Dad across the face," she says, and I lift my head in surprise.

"She did?"

"Hard. Left a handprint."

"Good for her." I sigh and lean against her again. "How could they do it?"

"Greed is a bitch," she says.

"I never pegged them for being greedy," I reply. "They said they were pissed that you and I got the money, and all they got was the house."

"Maybe Grandpa promised them more?" Lou suggests.

"Patrick gave House the letter before the reading of the will," I reply. "No, they were pissed and being greedy, and it makes me wonder how I didn't see it. I mean, these men *raised* us."

"Hey, there are men in the freaking mob who raise their kids and love them."

"Are you suggesting they're part of the mob?" I ask incredulously.

"No, I'm saying that sometimes people do bad things, but it doesn't make them bad people."

"I can't separate the two," I admit. "Not today."

"No, today is for being hurt. What are you going to do about Quinn?"

"I'm still hurt there too. So for now, I'm going to take some time to figure myself out and take it from there."

"Good idea," she says and goes back to playing with my hair, which has always calmed me. "I bet it wasn't easy for him to not tell you."

"He should have told me," I argue softly. "I know it's stupid, and I *know* better, but he should have told me. This was more than just a case."

"For you," she says.

"No, for both of us. I wasn't falling in love alone."

"Good point." Louise fills my glass with more wine. "We should probably move this party to Mom's. I don't want her to be alone."

"We'd better go before we're too buzzed to drive."

"Let's go."

Chapter Nineteen

~Quinn~

I know this road like the back of my hand. It's where I go when I'm upset, driving too fast through the thick trees.

Sunlight filters through the leaves onto the road as I speed away from the city, smoothly shifting through gears.

I'm pissed, and if I'm being perfectly honest, I'm hurt.

So I shift into fourth and rev the Porsche around a sharp turn, and right past a cop car.

"Fuck," I grumble as lights flash behind me and I pull over.

I don't have time for this. I *need* to drive, to burn off this anger and aggression.

I roll down my window, my license and insurance already in my hand.

"Did you know you were speeding?"

I glance up and want to smile. This is the same guy who

pulled me over years ago when I was driving the same road, after Dad died.

"Yes, sir," I reply honestly.

"Not just speeding, but going over a hundred in a fifty-five."

"Yes, sir."

"Have you been drinking?"

"No." I shake my head. "Just heartbroken like the last time you pulled me over. It's been a few years, you probably don't remember."

The cop shakes his head.

"Want me to get out and do the sobriety test?"

His eyes narrow now, but he steps away from the car. "Yes, please."

"Sure thing." I get out and immediately start walking the line.

"Something must have you upset," the cop says.

"Yeah, I'm pissed," I reply. "She says I lied to her, but I *didn't* lie. I couldn't tell her what I knew because it's attorney-client privilege. She's a damn attorney. She *knows* that."

I move into touching the tip of my nose with my finger.

"She found out today, before I could get to her and fill her in. My client finally gave me the green light, but she didn't have her phone on her, and I couldn't get to her first. She walked into a fucking shit show, in her own parents' house."

"That must have been tough," he says. I stand on one leg and touch my nose again.

"I can't even imagine," I agree. "Jesus, I wish I'd gotten to her first, or that I'd been with her."

"Would it have made a difference?" he asks. I turn, surprised to find him leaning against my car with his arms folded over his chest. He's an older man, probably in his late fifties. He looks like he's seen more than his fair share of shit.

"I don't know. And that's what guts me the most. The way she looked at me, with hollow eyes, and told me that she's done. We are *not* done. I refuse to let her shut me out of her life completely."

"Then why are you driving *away* from the city, rather than to her, to make her understand and hear you out?"

"I tried that already today," I admit with a sigh. "She was too upset to be reasonable. Hell, *I'm* too upset to be reasonable."

"And too upset to be driving on my road as fast as you were. I told you before, you could kill someone or yourself."

My eyes shift to his in surprise.

"Oh yeah, I remember you. You looked haunted then, like something was chasing you. Now you look defeated, and something tells me that you don't feel that way often."

"No." I shove my hands in my pockets and lean on the car next to him. "Are you going to give me a ticket?"

"No. But I'm going to give you some advice."

I give him a quizzical look, but stay quiet, curious to hear what he has to say.

"Now, I don't know all the facts, but I've been married for thirty-five years, and I've learned a thing or two about women and relationships. First of all, trust is a big thing."

"And I fucked that up," I murmur.

"Listening is important too," he says dryly, and I clamp my

mouth shut. "But the most important thing I've learned is to give her a minute to catch her breath. She's emotional right now, she's overthinking everything. And don't tell me she's not because most of us do."

I can only nod at that. Hell, I'm standing on a highway fifty miles outside of the city doing exactly that.

"We all need to feel safe. That the love, the trust, and the *heart* we put into each other is safe in our partner. Sounds to me like she's not feeling exactly safe in much right now."

"No. She's not."

"You need to fix that."

I stare at him. "How?"

"Well, every person's different, and like I said, I don't know the whole story, so you'll have to figure that out. Give her today to be mad, but don't let it fester for too long. If she's important to you, you need to get back in the ring and work for her."

"She's everything," I reply immediately. "She's the best part of my life."

"Then what are you doing racing away from her?"

I shake my head and shrug one shoulder. "Habit, I suppose."

"I think it's time to make some new habits, son."

I can't stand it anymore. I need to hear her voice.

I'm at the office, and it's been twenty-four hours since yesterday's fiasco. I'm trying to give her space, but I *need* her.

So I pick up my phone and dial her number. To my surprise, she answers on the second ring.

"Hello." She sounds exhausted.

"Hey." I sigh. "I wanted to let you know that I had all the boxes returned to your grandfather's house today."

"I know, I'm here now. Thanks for doing that so quickly."

"You're welcome." I swallow hard, hating the distance in her voice. "Sienna, I'm worried about you."

"I'm fine."

But I can hear that she's anything but fine.

"I don't want to lose you over this. I know that you're hurting, and I hate myself for causing that."

"You're not the only one who caused it," she interrupts. "It's turned into a shitty week."

"That might be the understatement of the century. You said yesterday that you're done."

"I'm not done with *us*." Her voice catches and my gut clenches. Jesus, I want to pull her into my arms and crush her to me. "I meant that I was done for the moment. That I need some time. I'm dealing with the arrest of my father and uncle, and my mom's a mess. So Lou and I are taking care of things, while also trying to keep our own professional lives afloat."

"I understand. Can I come help?"

"No, thank you." There's that catch again. "I need a little time, Quinn. Some space. I'm not done with us, I mean that, but the trust is bruised for me right now, even though the attorney in me understands what you did and why you did it. The woman in me needs a little time to catch up."

"Hurting you, deliberately hurting you, is never an option for me," I stress. "I tried so many times to think of a way to tell you without breaking the law."

"I don't think you could have," she whispers.

"Are you still going to Finn and London's engagement party with me on Friday?"

There's a long pause.

"I don't know. I'm not saying that to hurt you, Quinn. I'm not built like that."

I know she's not.

"But with my family falling apart, trying to catch up at work so I can take next week off, and everything else going on right now, I just don't think I can commit to anything. Not to mention, I'm not exactly wonderful company right now, and Finn and London's party should be full of excitement and love."

"They'll want you there," I reply. "*I* will want you there, so please think about it."

"I will."

"Sienna, I miss you. I love you *so much*, and I'm here whenever you need me and are ready for me to prove to you that something like this will never happen again."

She sniffles, and it breaks me.

"Baby, don't cry."

"I love you too." Her voice is breaking. "Thank you. I'll talk to you soon, okay, Quinn?"

"Okay."

She hangs up, and I'm left in my huge office, wondering how in the ever-loving fuck I'm going to fix this.

And then an idea starts to form.

I text Finn and Carter and ask them to come to my office ASAP.

I'm not disappointed when they both appear in less than two minutes.

"What's up?" Carter asks as they both have a seat.

"As you both know, yesterday was a shit show."

They nod in unison.

"Have you talked to her?" Finn asks.

"I just called her. The good news is, she hasn't written me off, but she also isn't ready to see me. She has a lot going on."

"I'm sure, what with half her family currently sitting in jail."

I push my hands through my hair in agitation.

"They deserve to be there," I retort, and Carter holds his hands up in surrender.

"I'm not saying they don't. But can you imagine if it were your parents in there?" We all shake our heads. "So what do you need?"

"I need to make it right. I know that I did the right thing for my career. But I did the wrong thing for Sienna."

"You didn't have a choice," Finn argues.

"I agree, and I hate to admit it, but I'd do it again. In a heartbeat. And because of that, I need to make sure that I never have to do it again."

"Agreed," Finn says.

"There are a few things going through my head right now," I continue, leaning forward to rest my elbows on the desk. "First,

I know we've talked about bringing in another partner to help shoulder some of the load."

Both of their eyebrows go up, and I hold my hands up.

"Just hear me out. Sienna is more than qualified, and we wouldn't offer her a partnership to start. But I would like to offer her a job. If she's working for the firm, I don't ever have to worry about keeping something from her professionally again."

"I understand," Carter says. "And if she wants to join the firm, I'm okay with that, but I'd like to hold off on a partnership until after she's been here for no less than three years."

"I agree," Finn says, and I nod.

"I can live with that. She may not want it, but I'd like to offer it to her. I hope I can talk her into it."

"Why wouldn't she want it? She'd be making a hell of a lot more money than she does for the city."

"She likes bankers' hours," I reply. "She paints and cooks and dedicates time to her family, so the city job has been perfect for her."

"That could be tough," Finn says. "We all work long hours."

"I get it, but again, I want to offer it to her. Hell, she could work part-time if she wants to. If she worked here, she could afford to."

"What else are you thinking over there?" Carter asks with a grin. "Besides getting in Sienna's pants?"

"I should deck you for that, but it's true and there's no time. Finn, can I use your beach house next week?"

"Sure. I'll have the caretaker open it up for you. Does that mean you'll be out of the office next week?"

"I hope so. Sienna just told me that she's taking next week off from work, and I'm hoping we can get away to the beach. And one more thing, I'm going to propose."

"What?" they ask in unison, both looking shocked.

"You heard me."

"I never thought I'd see the day," Finn murmurs. "When are you going to do it?"

"Well, that's where you come in. Here's my idea."

I'VE GIVEN HER two more days, and that's all I *can* give her.

It's late Thursday night. I haven't been home in days because being there reminds me of Sienna and how much I miss her.

She's ingrained herself in my home. Hell, she *is* my home.

And I'm damn tired of sleeping on the pullout couch in my office.

I pull up to her house, relieved to see that the light in her studio is still on, and without overthinking it or changing my mind, I walk up to the door and ring the doorbell.

She opens the door, a frown on her gorgeous, makeup-free face.

"Quinn? What are you doing here so late?"

"I know I said I'd give you space, but I can't stay away anymore, Sienna."

She steps back, letting me inside, and closes the door.

"Follow me," she says. She leads me to her studio. She's in her little shorts and tank, the ones that are full of paint spatters, but her hair is down around her face, and I can't help but smile at that.

She pads barefoot to the corner of her studio where she likes to paint, then points at the chair in the opposite corner.

"You can sit there while I finish this."

"Yes, ma'am."

As long as I get to be with her, I'll sit wherever she wants me.

She's finishing the big painting of the park that she started when our case began. It's in oils, and I now know what that means for her.

Turmoil. She paints in oils when she's upset, and I know that I've added to that.

It's killing me.

It only takes her about thirty minutes to finish what she's doing. She steps back, examining the painting as she cleans her brushes, and when it's all finished, she turns to me.

"It's finished."

"It's stunning." I mean that. The canvas is large, and the colors are bold. "You're so damn talented, Si."

"Thank you." She sighs and wipes a tear off her cheek. "I've about had enough of the tears."

"I hate it that you're hurt."

"The tears just come now, no matter what. It's like my tear ducts have been turned on and the faucet is broken. I can't get it to stop."

I take her hand and tug her onto my lap, bury my face in

her neck, and take a long, deep breath. "Jesus, I've missed you. I know we have a lot to work through, but I can't bring myself to spend another night away from you. Please don't send me away."

She wraps her arms around my neck and hugs me closely, presses a kiss to my temple, and then stands and takes my hand to lead me down to her bedroom.

I slip out of my clothes while Sienna washes up in the bathroom. There won't be any sex tonight.

I just need her against me, in my arms.

She walks into the bedroom, wearing only her panties and a clean tank, and we slide into bed, tangled up in each other.

There are a million things we need to talk about. Questions that need answers. But for tonight, I just want to hold her, to feel her against me, to know that we're going to come out the other side of this whole.

"I love you," I whisper. Her arm tightens around my stomach and she loops her leg over mine, hugging me with her whole body.

"I love you too. Is it still okay if I come to the party with you tomorrow night?"

I smile in the darkness.

"Sweetheart, you can do whatever you want."

"I'd like to come."

"Why the change of heart?"

"I need some happiness in my life right now," she admits. "And I really like Finn and London. I'm happy for them."

"They'll love having you there, and I'll be the luckiest man in the place."

"We have some things to talk about," she reminds me. "But not tonight."

"No." I kiss her head and feel her whole body let go of the tension she's been holding onto for the past four days. "Not tonight. Just sleep, love."

"I think Louise and I are going to go get pedicures in the morning," she says. Her voice is fading with slumber, but I'm happy to lie here and listen to her.

I've missed her more than I ever thought possible.

"That'll be fun."

"Mm. She's nervous about the party, so I want to be there for her too." She presses a sweet kiss to my shoulder. "And you. I've missed you too. I'm just stubborn."

"No." I smile into the darkness. "Not Sienna Hendricks."

"There's no need to be a smart-ass."

Chapter Twenty

~Sienna~

*O*h, we needed this," Louise says with a moan as the pedicurist scrubs the bottom of her feet. "They've been killing me, with all the walking I've been doing."

"That's one thing about being an event planner," I reply with a smile. "You'll be on your feet a lot."

"I need to get into better shape."

"Well, I'm proud of both my daughters," Mom says, watching us with misty eyes. She's been misty-eyed all week, just like me.

But I'm feeling *so much* better today. I haven't told them that Quinn came to stay with me last night, and I don't think I will.

I'm going to keep that just for me.

I hadn't been able to paint until last night either, and finishing the piece I started a month ago was important for me to be able to move forward. And Quinn showing up? Well, that was exactly the balm I needed to soothe me.

"Thanks again for helping out tonight, Mom," Louise says. "It'll be awesome to have you there; if nothing else, you can give me moral support. I know it's just an engagement party, not the actual wedding, but London is *famous*. There will be celebrities there, and this could get me some amazing contacts. In fact, London's already hired me to do the wedding."

"Oh my God." I reach over for Lou's hand. "I'm so proud of you. That's amazing. You're going to knock it out of the park."

"It helps that London isn't a bridezilla."

"What time is Quinn picking you up?" Mom asks.

"He's coming over at five," I reply and take a deep breath. Even though I saw him last night, and it felt wonderful, it doesn't mean that we don't need to have a pretty heavy conversation.

He was gone when I woke up this morning. I was sad that he didn't wake me to say good-bye. Maybe he thought it was for the best.

I'm excited to see him today, and to apologize. I owe him that.

"That's early," Lou says with a frown. "The party doesn't start until seven."

"We're going to talk." I shrug a shoulder. "We have some things to work through before we can move forward."

"Don't punish him anymore," Louise says.

"I'm not punishing him."

"Aren't you?" Mom asks. "You've talked with your father more than you've spoken with Quinn, and Quinn didn't do anything illegal."

"My father is *my father*, and he's in pretty deep trouble. I kind of had to talk to him."

"No, you didn't," Mom replies. "But you're a good person, Sienna."

"Let's just enjoy this pedicure and think about tonight," I suggest, wanting to change the subject. "What's for dinner, Lou?"

"We decided to do a buffet for this event, and a sit-down for the wedding." Louise goes into great detail, telling us all about the meal options tonight, how London insisted on serving Cristal for the toasts, and all the small details.

"I'm excited," Mom says. "It's going to be beautiful."

STOP PUNISHING HIM.

Is that what I've been doing? If so, it wasn't intentional. I needed some space to handle all the shit thrown at me this week.

I check the time. 4:55.

He'll be here any minute.

I bought a new green dress for this party. It complements my hair, and it fits my body well, with spaghetti straps and a long hemline with a slit up to my thigh. And, of course, I'm wearing the Louboutins that Quinn bought me.

I'm fastening my earrings when Quinn rings the bell. I open the door, and his jaw drops as his eyes travel from the top of my head all the way to the tips of my toes.

"Fuck."

"Not exactly what I was going for." His lips twitch as his eyes land on mine and he holds out a bouquet of fragrant flowers.

"For you."

"Thank you." I fuss over the blooms, burying my nose in them as I carry them to the kitchen for a vase. "These are beautiful."

"*You're* beautiful."

"Thank you," I repeat. I set the flowers on my dining table and turn to the sexiest man I know, who's decked out in a tux that fits him like a glove. "You look fantastic."

"It's the monkey suit."

"No, it's the man in it."

His eyes flare with lust and his hands curl into fists, but he doesn't come to me. Not yet.

"We need to talk," he begins and leans his hip on the countertop.

"I know."

"First of all, thank you for last night. We both needed it."

"We did." I cross my arms over my chest, but then worry that I'll wrinkle the dress, so I drop them. "I should have waited to put this on until *after* our talk."

"Are you uncomfortable?"

"I think I'd be uncomfortable no matter what I'm wearing."

"I don't want that," he says, shaking his head. His dark hair is teased back from his face, and he used some gel to keep it in place. "I don't ever want you to feel uncomfortable."

"Well, hopefully it won't last long. Quinn, I owe you an apology."

"No—"

"Let me finish. I *do* owe you an apology. You were doing

what you had to for your client, and for the law. I completely understand that. Frankly, I realize that I've been punishing you for something that I would have done myself."

"Sienna."

"I'm very sorry." My chin wobbles, which only pisses me off. "I wasn't going to cry when we did this." I clear my throat. "I'm not usually a crier."

"It's been a rough week," he says, and I *really* look at him. He looks tired.

"Yeah, it has. How are you?"

"Getting better by the minute." He flashes me that smile, the cocky one that I love so much, and my stomach loosens just a bit. "How is your mom?"

"She's okay. Confused. She's been beating herself up because she doesn't know how she missed what was happening under her own roof."

"It's not her fault."

"I know, and she knows it too, but it's tough. They've been married for almost forty years. I mean, I don't know what I would do if I were in her shoes."

"Is she sticking up for him?"

"No, but she hasn't left him either."

"Would you?"

"I'd like to say yes, but like I said, I don't know what I would do. They have forty years and two children between them. That would be hard to walk away from."

"Have you talked to them?"

I know exactly who *them* are.

"Not Patrick, and I won't. Not for a long while. I've seen my dad. They're both out on bail, and they probably won't see more jail time. I'm obviously not working this case for the city."

"Good."

"It's a conflict of interest, and my dad doesn't want me to work it because I'd put him in jail."

"You're angry."

"Fuck yes, I'm angry."

He nods, watching me from across the room.

"Are you done *not* touching me now?"

He's across the room in less than a second, his arms wrapped around me in a tight hug. My ear is pressed to his chest and I can hear his heart beating fast.

"I missed you," I murmur. "And I know there's more to talk about, but—"

"But it's enough for today," he finishes for me before pressing his lips to mine. "Now, let's go enjoy some of that happiness you were talking about last night."

"Excellent plan."

"This party is *amazing*," I say to London a few hours later, after the toasts and we've all stuffed ourselves to the gills with incredible food.

"Louise is the *best*. Thank you for suggesting her. She told me that she's starting a business, and I think that I'll keep her busy with my wedding and some of my friends' parties as well."

"That's awesome, thank you."

"She earned it." London clinks her glass to mine, and the music changes to a soft slow song that I love by Rob Thomas.

Suddenly, Quinn is standing before me, holding his hand out for mine.

"Dance with me?"

"Sure."

London takes my drink and I walk to the dance floor with my man. He tugs me into his arms, slowly leading me across the floor.

"You have an easy way about you," I say. "On the dance floor, that is."

"Are you saying I'm not easy off the dance floor?"

"That's what I'm saying." I grin and thread my fingers through his hair at the nape of his neck. "But it would be boring if you were easy."

"I'm glad you feel that way."

We leave our pieces on the ground . . .

The song is swirling around us. No one else is dancing, which is kind of weird, but I'm so caught up in the music, and dancing with Quinn, that I don't think much of it.

"You are everything to me, Sienna."

His voice is strong and commanding. I look up into his eyes and catch my breath.

Quinn is an intense man.

"You are the best part of every day. You're my home. You make me a better man. I know we haven't been together for long, but I don't do anything slow or halfway."

A smile tickles his lips and every hair on my body stands on end.

"I live my life in the fast lane. I like it there. But it's nothing without you in it with me, every single day."

He reaches into his jacket and pulls out a ring, and my hand covers my open mouth in absolute shock.

Quinn drops to one knee as the whole room quiets. The music is gone, and all eyes are on us, listening with bated breath.

"Marry me, sweetheart. Be my partner, my companion, my love. I swear to you, there won't ever be a dull moment."

I'm caught up in his eyes, in the sincerity there, and the confidence in the way he's holding my hand.

Quinn is my rock. My constant. And I know I don't want to do this life without him.

"Yes."

The room explodes in whoops and whistles, and Quinn catches me up in a fierce hug, then plants his lips on mine and kisses me until Finn yells out, "Get a room!"

I glance around, surprised to see not only my mom and Louise holding hands and crying, but Rich too. We're surrounded by excited family, wanting to see the ring, and congratulate us, but I'm still caught in Quinn's gaze, trying to soak it in.

"I'm getting married."

"Damn right you are," Lou says before hugging me. "And I get to plan it."

WE'VE BEEN AT the beach for three days, and I don't ever want to go home.

Quinn had studio supplies set up for me, and I've spent hours painting watercolors: of the ocean and of London's beach house for their engagement gift.

I brought my pencil and paper down to the beach to do a rough sketch. I haven't used pencil before, but I think it could be something fun to try.

Quinn's taught me that it's worth it to try new things.

But I keep getting distracted by the light on my ring. I know, it sounds cheesy, but Quinn didn't skimp on this rock. It's a princess cut, must be two karats, and fits my finger perfectly.

He says we'll get something fancy for the wedding band, but I think he's nuts. This is plenty fancy for me.

"Hey there, pretty girl."

I glance up, shielding my eyes from the sun, and smile when I see Quinn walking toward me, wearing his signature cargo shorts and T-shirt.

"Hey yourself."

"Are you about done?"

"Just finishing up."

"Good because I'm hungry."

I grin and walk with him into the house where I've had chili simmering all afternoon. While it's still summer, it's cooler at the beach, and I've been hungry for a pot of chili.

"I just have to whip up the cornbread."

"How long will that have to bake?"

"About thirty minutes."

A slow smile slides over his face. "Not quite as long as I was hoping for, but I'll take it."

"You're incorrigible."

"When it comes to my fiancée? Absolutely."

Fiancée.

Am I ever going to get used to that? Probably not.

"So I've been thinking," Quinn says as he opens the lid of the pot on the stove and gives it a stir. "Damn, this smells good."

"What are you thinking?"

"Come work at the firm."

I slip the cornbread into the oven, then turn to stare at Quinn.

"Right." I laugh and shake my head, certain that he's joking.

"I'm serious."

"Quinn, I'm not quitting my city job. You know that I love it there."

"I know you love the *hours* there," he replies. "Here's the thing, Si. I can't ever be in the same situation that I was in with Bruce. I *can't* withhold information from you. It made me crazy."

"And I love you for that, I do. But there are other ways. For one thing, we make sure that we aren't ever opposing counsel again. I work in the Bronx, and you work in Manhattan. The odds of that happening again are extremely low."

"That's the other thing," he continues. "I don't love the idea of that commute for you."

"You mean for you?"

His mouth opens and closes like a fish on land, and I secretly laugh.

"Who says I'm the one who has to move?"

He pushes his hand through his hair. "Well, I hadn't considered that we'd live anywhere but the condo. Don't you like the condo?"

"Sure, I like it. I also like my house."

His eyes narrow. "Okay."

"Okay what?"

"I guess I'm commuting."

I blink quickly. "Just like that?"

"Sienna, haven't you figured it out? As long as I'm with you, I don't give a fuck where we live. *You* are home. It doesn't matter what the address is."

"You'd give up your fancy condo for me."

"Well, to be fair, I probably wouldn't sell it." He shrugs as I let out a loud laugh. "But if you want to live in your house, fine."

I can't hold myself back any longer. I rush to him and launch myself into his arms. He catches me easily, his hands planted on my ass and my legs wrapped around his waist, as he kisses me senseless.

He backs me against the wall, grinding himself against my core, and I gasp.

"I had you this morning, and I want you as if I haven't had you in months."

"Same," I breathe, reaching between us to unfasten his shorts. Finally, we're stripped bare, and he pushes inside me, making us both gasp in ecstasy.

"God, I'll never get tired of the way you feel," he growls against my neck. He's holding me up with one hand, the other is planted on the wall beside my head, and he's moving in a fast, steady rhythm that makes my eyes cross. "You're so fucking amazing."

"It's us," I say breathlessly, holding on for dear life. My toes are clenched, my fingers tight in his hair, and he changes it up, pulling out of me, setting me on my feet and spinning me face-first against the wall. He bites my shoulder, where it meets my neck, and I see stars.

"Damn right it's us," he says, kissing his way down my back to my rear, where he sinks his teeth into my cheek. "Have I told you how much I love these dimples above your ass?"

"I don't think so."

"Well, I do." He presses a kiss to each of them, and then he's standing behind me again, the head of his cock pressed to me. Every time I think I've never been more ready for him, and then it happens again and I'm even *wetter* than before. How is that even possible? "I love everything about you."

The rhythm is faster now. He's a man driven to make me completely crazy, and it's working. My legs shake as I come apart, and he calls out my name as he falls over the edge with me, just as the timer dings on the oven.

"Good timing," he says with a grin. He kisses me softly, completely opposite of the frenzied lovemaking from just a few moments ago. "I'm hungry."

"Me too."

I pull my clothes on and take the pan of cornbread out of the oven.

"So what do you say about the job?" he asks.

"Oh, we never finished that conversation, did we?"

"No."

"You work an insane number of hours, Quinn. I'm not afraid of hard work, not in the least, but—"

"Come on part-time," he suggests and cuts himself a bite of the hot cornbread. I'm too surprised to tell him hands off. "Then even if you're working extra now and then, it's still within the number of hours you want to work."

"You know, I have excellent benefits at the city."

"You'd have better benefits at the firm."

He wiggles his eyebrows, making me laugh.

"Let me think about it."

"Do that. The offer's always open. So . . . we're going to live in the Bronx?"

"Oh, no. We're totally living at your condo, I just wanted to see your reaction when I said I wanted to stay at the house."

"*Our* condo," he says, and then swats me on the butt with the palm of his hand. "Smart-ass."

"Get used to it, ace. It is what it is."

"Never a dull moment," he says, repeating what he said the other night, which only reignites the excitement in my belly.

No, life's not going to be dull. It's going to be thrilling, and fun, and maybe a little scary sometimes.

And you know what? I can't fucking wait.

About the Author

KRISTEN PROBY has published close to forty titles, many of which have hit the *USA Today, New York Times*, and *Wall Street Journal* bestsellers lists. She continues to self-publish, best known for her With Me In Seattle and Boudreaux series, and is also proud to work with William Morrow, a division of HarperCollins, with the Fusion and Romancing Manhattan series.

Kristen and her husband, John, make their home in her hometown of Whitefish, Montana, with their two cats.

BOOKS BY KRISTEN PROBY

LISTEN TO ME
A Fusion Novel; Book One

Five best friends open a hot new restaurant, but one of them gets much more than she bargained for when a sexy former rock star walks through the doors-and into her heart.

CLOSE TO YOU
A Fusion Novel; Book Two

Since the day she met Landon Palazzo, Camilla LaRue, part owner of the wildly popular restaurant Seduction, has been head-over-heels in love. And when Landon joined the Navy right after high school, Cami thought her heart would never recover. Now, Landon is back and he looks better than ever.

BLUSH FOR ME
A Fusion Novel; Book Three

When Kat, the fearless, no-nonsense bar manager of Seduction, and Mac, a successful but stubborn business owner, find themselves unable to play nice or even keep their hands off each other, it'll take some fine wine and even hotter chemistry for them to admit they just might be falling in love.

THE BEAUTY OF US
A Fusion Novel; Book Four

Riley Gibson is over the moon at the prospect of having her restaurant, Seduction, on the Best Bites TV network. This could be the big break she's been waiting for. But the idea of having an in-house show on a regular basis is a whole other matter. And when she meets Trevor Cooper, the show's executive producer, she's stunned by their intense chemistry.

SAVOR YOU
A Fusion Novel; Book Five

Cooking isn't what Mia Palazzo does, it's who she is. She's built a stellar menu for her restaurant, Seduction. Now, after being open for only a few short years, Mia's restaurant is being featured on Best Bites TV. Then Camden Sawyer, the biggest mistake of her life, walks into her kitchen... As Mia and Camden face off, neither realizes how high the stakes are as their reputations are put on the line and their hearts are put to the ultimate test.

ALL THE WAY
Romancing Manhattan, Book 1

Three brothers get more than they bargain for as they practice law, balance life, and navigate love in and around New York City.